Write a Novel
in
Eight Weeks

Cenarth Fox

The raison d'être

Let's say we can divide the would-be novelists of the world into three groups.

(a) People who talk about writing a novel. 'I'm going to write a novel one day.'
(b) People who start to write a novel. 'I'm up to chapter 3.'
(c) People who finish writing their novel and publish it. 'Here is a copy of my novel.'

The raison d'être of this book is about getting you into the third category; people who finish writing their novel and publish it.

The abiding principle

In the world of writing, apart from, "Thou must be interesting", there are no rules.

A bird's-eye view of the course

Weeks 1 - 8
Choose genre, title, write elevator pitch and wall sign
Write plot
Write first draft of novel between 40,000 and 50,000 words

Weeks 9-11
Edit your novel
Publish your novel as print or an eBook or both

Table of Contents

Introduction

While this book is aimed at writers who wish to complete their first novel, it is not only for beginners. Writers who have already published a novel or novels, who wish to improve their writing skills or want someone or something to give them a shove to get another novel done and dusted, should find ideas and inspiration in this book.

And it is not exclusively for novelists. Many of the tips can apply to other forms of writing such as memoir and non-fiction.

This course is divided into five parts – plan, pen, polish, publish and promote. You will learn how to plan your work, how to pen it, to polish, publish and promote it.

The final format of your manuscript can be in print form (paperback or hardback), or in electronic form, i.e. an eBook. It could even be an audio book.

WARNING. You must do the heavy lifting. There is information and guidance galore but the job of producing the content, writing the words of your novel, is all down to you.

This book is based on the course *Write a Novel in Eight Weeks* devised and taught by Cenarth Fox at the U3A, the University of the Third Age, in Melbourne, Australia.

Write a Novel in Eight Weeks
© Cenarth Fox 2024
ISBN 978-0-949175-74-8
Published by FOX PLAYS
https://www.foxplays.com
https://www.cenfoxbooks.com

Cover illustration by Oliviaprodesign

Here's the Fine Print

This book is about you writing the first draft of a novel between 40,000 and 50,000 words in eight weeks. You could finish your first draft in less time. And once you finish your first draft, you have three weeks to edit, polish and publish your novel.

But why rush to finish a novel in such a relatively short time?

You don't have to rush. It's not compulsory. This is a voluntary exercise. But it can be done and if you want to break free from taking forever to write your novel, and, at the same time, improve your writing skills, and learn how to publish your novel, this is an excellent way to get the job done. I've proved it works with my own writing as have my students.

It's true some novelists can take forever to write their novel. But if the course in this book is followed, you could be holding your finished work in under three months.

By putting yourself under reasonable but healthy pressure, you lift your game. You develop self-discipline which in turn becomes a habit. Good habits are great habits. And as the daily milestones are passed, your confidence grows. You delight in self-satisfaction. You feel better about yourself and delight in seeing your novel come to life.

Finally, one of the best ways to improve as a writer is to write. You get better at doing it by doing it. You make mistakes and learn from them. Your writing skills continue to improve.

Mind you this course carries additional benefits. It's not only about having the finished story completed on time, but also about gaining writing skills. You will discover tips you can apply during the writing of your novel and in the future.

But why the future? Because once you complete the novel you're about to write, you may well be keen to get cracking on the next and the next. Success breeds success, enthusiasm breeds enthusiasm.

Okay, but what if it's terrible?

What if my novel is poor, even seriously bad? In the beginning it almost certainly will be. A first draft can be described as both the best and the worst version of your novel. It's the best because it exists – you can't re-write what you haven't written. And it's the worst because if you've written it the way a first draft should be written, flat out, no looking back, then it's likely to be liberally laced with typos, repetition, irrelevancies and good old-fashioned crappiness. Welcome to the first-draft writers' club.

What's the timetable?

You spend eight weeks writing the first draft of your novel which has between 40,000 and 50,000 words. Seriously? Are you saying a novelist can nominate the number of words in their finished novel *before* they start to write? I am. But how? More on that later.

If you work hard, you might finish your first draft in less than eight weeks. Good for you. And if you do finish ahead of schedule, that will give you more time to re-write and publish. But this course uses 8 weeks to write and 3 weeks to re-write and publish.

What's the deal with the publishing?

Here are four ways to publish your novel. In this course you learn about all four types and concentrate on how to become a self-publisher.

- ✓ Traditional
- ✓ Hybrid
- ✓ Vanity
- ✓ Self

You will learn to self-publish a print book and an eBook. You can publish either or both.

Many people would like to write a novel and have it published by someone else. Being offered a contract by a traditional publisher sounds and is terrific. If that happens, you'll be skipping around your loungeroom waving the offer as you celebrate.

A traditional publisher will handle everything - the editing, design, printing, distribution, the launch and marketing. You become excited, start your next novel and wait for the royalties to roll in. You may even receive an advance. This is where the publisher pays the author money once the book is launched. The publisher retains all income from the sales of your book until the advance is reached after which you receive royalties from future sales. Sounds good. *Is* good.

A fact of life is that traditional publishers receive far more manuscripts than they publish. Most novels are either self-published or published by vanity or hybrid publishers. More on them later. In this course, the chosen method is self-publishing.

You are the publisher

Once your first draft and editing work is complete, as a self-publisher, you choose how it appears. Here are your options.

✓ You print it yourself to create a physical book.
✓ You have a print business print it for you to create a physical book.
✓ You upload it to a publisher such as Amazon as a physical or eBook or both.

If printed, your novel could be a hardback or paperback (soft cover). If not printed, it could be an eBook or an audio book. More on these possibilities later.

How to write a specific number of words

I don't think many novelists start writing a novel aiming to reach a certain number of words. After much editing, the final word count is what it is. But there are ways to help you write a specific number, and in this case it's between 40K and 50K. To do so, follow these rules.

✓ One or two main characters
✓ Few minor characters
✓ One main theme or event
✓ One sub-plot, minor not major
✓ A restricted time in which the action takes place. A short novel can be set over a day, week, a month or even several months.

Why Eight Weeks?

Yes, why not nine or ten weeks? It's all about the raison d'être listed at the front of this book. We want, need, *must* land in category (c). We want to finish our novel. If the target word count is 60K, 80K or 100K, eight weeks would be nigh on impossible. We choose a shorter time to suit a shorter novel. The prize at the end of this course is your finished novel. So, let's do the maths.

To write a first draft of 40K words in eight weeks, you need to average about seven hundred words a day. If your first draft is 50K, then that daily word count is more like nine hundred words a day. Likewise, 45K words would require an average of about eight hundred words a day. How does that make you feel?

In teaching the contents of this book in a class of budding novelists, no two students were the same. Several had been writing for decades, some could touch type, some had already drafted a novel or novels, and some struggled to tackle the subject, lacking confidence and wanting guidance. Everyone is unique.

But here is a plan, a method to allow you to complete a polished and published novel in under three months. If that appeals, give it a go. Give it a go anyway. And remember, once you start, you can already see the finishing line. It's not way off in the distance, it's close getting closer.

Tell me again, what is the point of finishing a lousy novel?

There is no point other than you should improve your skills in the process. We can all learn from our mistakes. But in this course, the basic assumption is only your best work will do. This book always assumes your novel will be highly polished. And to help you achieve that status, there are teaching points to improve the quality and many details on how to edit your work.

When it comes to writing a novel, I never like to use, see or hear the word *easy*. Nothing about writing is easy. Mind you, promoters of AI software would beg to differ. If anyone tells you writing, editing and marketing a novel is easy, they're fibbing. It is *never* easy.

Mind you *talking* about writing a novel is easy. But we don't talk, we write.

If you follow the steps in this book, the tips provided, you should reach category (c). To do that, to achieve success, I reckon you need two qualities: knowledge and determination. I can help with the knowledge, but the determination bit is all down to you.

Do you need qualifications and training to write a novel?

No, although any relevant course can help. This book explains the mistakes a novelist might make and shows how you can recognize and avoid them. It points out shortcuts to help you improve the writing and re-writing of your novel.

Perhaps your most important quality is determination. Not only is writing a novel not easy, but it can also be, no *is* damn hard work. Some writers will tell you it's a slog. To be forewarned is to be forearmed. Be prepared for the hard work involved. Keep going. What is that saying by Thomas Edison?

> *"Genius is 1 per cent inspiration and 99 per cent perspiration."*

It can be done. You can succeed. By the end of this book, you can hold a published copy of your first or latest novel.

What happens if I don't finish on time?

Nothing. The sun will come up tomorrow and life will go on.

You may get to week eleven and not be ready to publish. That's not the end of the world. But the experience of most of the students I worked with on this course, saw them break the back of their novel writing and editing leaving them close to achieving their goal. And the experience was invaluable as they improved their writing skills.

Okay, you might need a week or three after Week 11, big deal. Keep going with what you've been doing and enter category (c). This programme works and you can succeed.

Welcome budding novelist.

As you work through this book, feel free to make notes if anything needs further study or explanation or if you find a practical hint you want to use in your work.

Happy reading and writing.

Cenarth Fox

A bit about the author

My first name, Cenarth, is Welsh. There is no K in the Welsh alphabet meaning, in Welsh, the letter C is hard as in *cake* and never soft as in *circle*. Cenarth is pronounced Kenarth. Most people call me Cen which is pronounced Ken.

I've been a primary and secondary school teacher teaching English and Music. I've self-published plays, musicals, novels and non-fiction books. I've written novels in various genres – historical fiction, thrillers, crime, biographical fiction, romance and children's. More details about my books at https://www.cenfoxbooks.com

Explanations

As you work through this book, certain topics or words may seem strange or unknown. If you know the meaning, great, keep going. If you're not sure, pause and learn. Make a note of anything unknown. Oh, and there's a dictionary of sorts at the back of the book. Here's an example.

First draft. A novel (and other writing projects or activities) is rarely written and ready for publication in one go. I think *never* is better than *rarely*. Re-writing will always be required. When you finish the first version of your novel, that edition or version is called the first draft or the rough draft.

Now let's crack on with defining a novel – the one you're about to write.

"There is something delicious about writing the first words of a story. You never quite know where they'll take you."
Beatrix Potter

Chapter 1
What is a novel?

In simple terms a novel is a made-up story, an invented tale. Books can be roughly divided into fiction and non-fiction. Here we're aiming to write fiction. We invent the characters and the plot and tell the story.

Novels have been written for thousands of years. They come in different lengths, in different genres, and in different styles.

Speaking of different lengths, here we are talking about a novel between 40,000 and 50,000 words. Okay, so what will be the length of your masterpiece? Good question because the length of your novel is the key to your success in this course.

Did you know the famous novel *War and Peace* by Tolstoy has more than half a million words? The author stated, "It is not a novel" so here we bump into an important word in this book, an important word full stop.

subjective – a subjective opinion is one based on a personal belief or feeling. It's the opposite to an objective opinion which is not based on personal feelings but on facts. You can argue that *subjective* may be biased whereas *objective* is not.

Tolstoy reckoned he produced "a literary work" and here we have an example of an opinion; his and others because some people do describe *War and Peace* as a novel.

So, what is a definition of a novel?

It's a narrative of a certain length, usually prose, with characters and action involving some type of realism. That's not to say the characters must be human or the action must be set on planet Earth. And the time of your novel can be the present, the past or the future.

Speaking of word count or the length of your novel, this book aims to help you produce a novel which is way, way shorter than *War and Peace*. Eight weeks to produce a first draft with 700,000 words is laughable. That works out at more than 12,000 words a day every day for 56 days. Phew!

So, let's reinforce the length of the novel you are aiming to write according to this book.

I suggest 40,000 to 50,000 words.

Now immediately issues arise. Can you start writing a novel knowing how long it will be by the time you finish? I don't think you can, at least certainly not an exact amount. But the rules listed earlier (page 3) will seriously corral the number of words in your novel.

Fewer characters, a single theme or event and a shortish time, means you have a darn good chance of writing a first draft of between 40 and 50 thousand words in 8 weeks.

I've done it and so have some of my students.

Types of fiction

Short Story: Fewer than 7,500 words
Novelette: 7,500 – 17,500 words
Novella: 17,500 – 40,000 words
Novel: 50,000+ words (Some, like me, say 40K+)

So, is a book with 44,444 words a novel or a novella?

Here we bump into that word again – *subjective*. The definitions above are not set in stone. Some believe a work of fiction must have at least 50,000 words before it can be called a novel while others argue 40,000 words gives it the novel tick.

Are you writing a novel or a novella?

Test your idea to see if you are preparing to write a novel or novella, i.e. fewer than 40K. If you have little detail, you might even be planning to write a short story. How can you tell?

On a single page, list the events to occur in your "novel". This is a pre-plot of your plot. Can you use the bones of your story to create a novel of at least 40,000 words? If not, you could enter the room marked, "Stuff in extra words". Don't do that. This is where your short story or novella is padded to make it a novel. Avoid it. Padding within a novel should be removed without prejudice.

It's tricky to guess the possible word count but if the event/s in your one-page plot can be told in 15 or even 20 thousand words, then you are not writing a novel. Again, how can you tell? An experienced novelist can make an educated guess with approximate word count details. If you're inexperienced, it can be a steep learning curve. Here's an idea.

Read some short stories and short novels. Does your idea fit into what you've read? The important thing is to be aware of your novel being at least 40,000 words.

Quotes to ponder

"What makes you a writer? Writing makes you a writer. Being a writer says nothing about how good you are, how prolific you are, whether you are published or not. When you write you are a writer. When you don't, you aren't. So, practice your craft and proudly call yourself a writer." **Melanie Anne Phillips**

"Get through a draft as quickly as possible." **Joshua Wolf Shank**

"Read a lot and write a lot.
Avoid adverbs.
Remove the unnecessary.
Try to write every day.
Use simple words."
Stephen King

"I learned to write by writing."
Neil Gaiman

"The road to hell is paved with works-in-progress."
Philip Roth

"Writing is hard, but the more you write, and enjoy what you write, the better it gets."
Alice Munro

To write is human, to edit is divine."
Stephen King

"Good writing is essentially rewriting."
Roald Dahl

"There is no great writing, only great rewriting."
Louis D Brandeis

"The desire to write grows with writing."
Desiderius Erasmus

"If you wish to be a writer, write."
Epictetus

"If a story is in you, it has to come out."
William Faulkner

Word count of some well-known novels

The Lion, The Witch, and the Wardrobe 36,363 words
Lord of the Flies 59,900 words (approx.)
The Great Gatsby 47,093 words (approx.)
War and Peace 587,287 words
The Hound of the Baskervilles 28,000 words (approx.)
David Copperfield 360,231 words
Murder on the Orient Express 84,000 words (approx.)

If the argument states that 50,000 words is the minimum word count for a novel, then some famous novels listed above have changed category and become a novella.

The three parts of a novel

Most novels are divided into three parts – the beginning, the middle and the end.

Beginning
25%
Grab the reader

Middle
50%
Pacing's important

End
25%
Resolve

The size of the parts, the percentages, are flexible, approximate and those above are roughly correct. It is usual to have a beginning and an end both of which are smaller in word count size than the middle. The middle, ah the middle, is usually the biggest part. Each part is important. Your novel is like a chain being only as strong as its weakest link. If one part of your novel is muddled or messy, you negate your other two brilliant parts.

Like the three parts of a novel, this book too, is divided into three parts.

Plot or Pants
One or the other

Prose
Writing your novel

Polish/Publish
Re-write, re-write, re-write

Explanation

Many but not all novelists create a plot, (sometimes called a plan or an outline) before they start to write their novel. It's a blueprint or a guide. They constantly refer to their plot as they write the first draft of their novel.

But not all novelists follow this routine. Some dive right in and start writing. They don't have a plot or, at best, a minor or sketchy one. They let the story develop being led by their imagination, their next thought or idea. These novelists are said to be flying by the seat of their pants. They are pantsers or are pantsing.

Should I be a Plotter or a Pantser?

You decide. I'm a plotter and have never tried pantsing. I find it scary to simply start writing a novel without a plot be that sketchy or detailed. In a murder mystery, I need to know certain things - whodunit, details of the victim, the murder method, how the mystery was solved and much more. I assume the pantser doesn't need any of that and simply starts.

"It was a dark and stormy night."

I don't know if this is a true story, but I've heard the great novelist, Agatha Christie, would not choose the character who committed the murder until the penultimate chapter. She would give several characters the ability to commit the deed but not select the perpetrator until almost the end. If true, it's a fascinating way to plot your novel.

But I am often a pantser when writing such things as an article, a blog post or an editorial. Such a piece of writing might be only a few hundred words, if that. But when writing a novel with 80,000 words, I need a blueprint, a plan, a plot.

So, this is one of many decisions you must make when starting to write the first draft of your novel over a period of eight weeks. Are you a plotter or a pantser? More on plotting later, much more.

Chapter 2
Explain the Maths

Why Eight Weeks?

Arguably the best way to achieve your goal of finishing a novel including its publication within 11 weeks is to climb a hill rather than a mountain. By limiting the number of words in your novel, you set yourself a realistic goal for the time allowed.

This book could change its title to *Write a Novel in 12 Weeks* or *24 Weeks* or longer and for such a course, the approach to help you write, and the tips would be the same. But writing and publishing a 45,000-word novel in 3 months is, I argue, less of a challenge. Remember nothing in writing is easy. Eight weeks is chosen to push you, to increase the chances of you getting the job done and on time.

Think of it this way. Having a timetable of eight weeks to complete your first draft means you can see the finishing line ahead. You are not starting a journey which could take months even years. You're not writing some massive tome wondering where you're up to during the project. This way you can gauge your progress at any time, on every day. And if you stick to your routine, after eight weeks, you can be ready to polish and publish.

This course gives you eight weeks to complete your first draft, and three weeks to edit, to polish and finally to publish. It sounds tricky, even difficult, but it has and can be done.

The maths

You have eight weeks to write your first draft
This equals 56 days
To write the first draft of a 50,000-word novel, you need to write about 900 words a day
To write the first draft of a 40,000-word novel, you need to write about 700 words a day
You could produce more than the average number of words per day
You could complete your first draft in less time e.g. 5, 6 or 7 weeks

Some factors to consider

We're human and looking at the numbers above, an average of 700 words a day is not impossible, but there are factors to consider. Have you written much before? Writing essays, non-fiction and other writing activities can help. Are you a touch typist? Experience and skills can make a difference. Then other factors such as health and commitments? What are your responsibilities which take precedence over your writing? Are you a student, a worker, a volunteer or a retiree? Everyone's situation is unique.

Here is an idea to help you reach your goal

Find a writing buddy or buddies. This is someone who knows about your writing activity. They might be doing the same or a similar thing. Being able to chat in person or online with a fellow novelist or novelists has great potential. FaceTime and Zoom can help here.

- ✓ You can encourage one another
- ✓ You can share problems and find a sympathetic voice
- ✓ You can have questions answered or answer questions from someone else
- ✓ You can write more wanting to keep up with your fellow wordsmith

Tip

Join an online novel writing project.
NaNoWriMo – https://www.nanowrimo.org (It's free)
NaNoWriMo stands for National Novel Writing Month (November)

This is a supportive platform for writers who want to write a novel, even their first. You can set milestones, track your progress, connect with fellow writers in a vast community, and participate in events designed to help you complete your novel. It's free and may give your writing a serious boost. Check it out.

Chapter 3
Before you Start Writing

GOOD ADVICE at the beginning is to hasten slowly. Here are three things you need *before* you start your novel writing. Even a pantser should at least consider these items.

1. Select a genre
2. Write an elevator pitch
3. Create a wall sign

A fourth item is a title or at least a working title. You don't want to refer to your novel as "my novel" or "that thing". Give it a name, an identity. You can change it later if you wish.

In novel writing, a genre is a category defined by its form, style or content. Each genre has certain characteristics. Here are some genres of novels. It is not a complete list. Amazon lists thousands of genres. Here are some popular ones.

mystery, romance, fantasy, crime, historical fiction, thriller, science fiction, horror, action and adventure, women's fiction, LGBTQ+, contemporary, literary fiction, YA, children's.

There are sub-genres within a genre. Discover more at [The Ultimate List of Book Genres: 35 Popular Genres (reedsy.com)](reedsy.com) There's even a quiz to help you discover your genre.

Time to Choose

To be a plotter or a pantser is one thing. To pick a genre is another. It is not optional. You really should choose a genre even if your novel has a mix of genres. I mean you could have a romance in a thriller or a murder in a science fiction novel.

My advice is to choose a genre you like or have read often. Of course, many successful authors say to be a novelist you must be a reader.

"Writing comes from reading, and reading is the finest teacher of how to write."
Annie Proulx

"Read, read, read. Read everything—trash, classics, good and bad, and see how they do it. Just like a carpenter who works as an apprentice and studies the master. Read! You'll absorb it. Then write. If it's good, you'll find out. If it's not, throw it out of the window."
William Faulkner

So is your novel a thriller, a romance, science fiction, fantasy or what? Choose a genre and know its characteristics. How? Do some research. Look for "Characteristics of a Thriller" or of a romance or science fiction or ... etc.

Having chosen your genre, you need two more things: an elevator pitch and a wall sign.

Okay, you pantsers will say they can ignore an elevator pitch and possibly even a wall sign because they are making up their novel on the fly. That may be true but think about it before abandoning the issues. You can write an elevator pitch and still be a pantser.

In some countries, an elevator is a lift, a box which carries people up and down a building with many floors. In an elevator pitch, a pitch is a speech, a short presentation where the speaker, a novelist, is trying to convince a person of influence, the CEO of a traditional publishing company, why their idea for a novel is super cool and deserves to be published.

An Elevator Pitch Explained

Use your imagination and suspend disbelief. An author enters an elevator with the CEO of a major publisher. The literary big wig is heading to their office on the 32nd floor. The author has between the beginning and end of the journey to pitch their novel. The whole point of your EP is to force you to explain your about-to-be-written novel in a short time.

Now we're not talking reality here. I doubt if many publishing bosses have been accosted in an elevator by an enthusiastic author. The normal process is to find a literary agent who will approach a publisher on your behalf although not necessarily in a lift.

Here's a sad fact. Just as there are far more novels written than are accepted by a traditional publishing house, so too literary agents get far more requests from authors than they, the agent, can handle. I once saw a literary agent explaining how she might get up to 200 requests a year from authors, and from that number she takes on probably two new clients, perhaps three in a Leap Year.

So, the purpose of you writing your elevator pitch before you start to even plot your novel is not for the benefit of some CEO from an international publisher; it's for you. It's to help you have a clear vision of what your novel is all about.

Once you've finished your novel and polished it till it shines, you can hang out in the foyer of a tall building waiting for the head of the publishing company. No, don't bother with that. Find an agent or make your pitch to the company's gatekeeper.

gatekeeper – a person who first encounters a manuscript sent to a publisher. The gatekeeper has the power to reject said manuscript before it even gets to first base. Now your pitch must be short and clear. Hopefully it will be interesting even riveting. Remember this is for <u>your</u> benefit. Here are some elevator pitch rules.

- ✓ Keep it under 100 words
- ✓ No names of characters
- ✓ Finish with a cliff-hanger

A Wall Sign

Like an elevator pitch, (the EP), a wall sign too is for your benefit. It's a mini-EP. It can be words or a picture. Its purpose is to help you finish your novel in 8 weeks. How?

It keeps you focused on your stated goal. Don't wander off on a side road. Don't let a sub-plot become the main plot. A clear, succinct wall sign keeps you on track. Make a wall sign.

As the name suggests, a wall sign is a sign you place on a wall meaning you can't miss it. If your wall sign is in a clear line of sight, you will stare or look at it every time you sit down to write, even as you write. It will reinforce what your novel is all about. Keep the message on the sign simple.

Example

I wrote a 49,000-word novel in 8 weeks, and polished and published said novel in three weeks, a total of eleven weeks. Here are the three things I created.

Genre
Romance

Sub-genre
Seniors

Elevator Pitch
A surprising, wonderful and unexpected romance blooms for two seniors despite their love struggling to survive. Family members turn nasty to kill the union and when a life and death event explodes, a happy ending seems doomed. Will love triumph?

I changed the wall sign for a monitor picture.

The covers below are in full colour although this book is printed in black and white hence the lack of colour apart from the cover. In the eBook version of this book, every colour graphic is shown in all its glory.

Wall sign

I didn't create a wall sign. Instead, I produced a rough cover of my novel, which I placed as a screen saver on my monitor. Every time I turned on my machine, there were the two main characters of my novel. A picture can be an alternative to a wall sign. Had I chosen a wall sign, it might have been something like this.

Seniors in Love
or
A Santa Romance
or
Love for Oldies

Of course, the cover of your novel is important and there's plenty of information on that topic later. And for a professional-looking cover, I hired a designer and my humble effort above was replaced by the following.

I plan to write a second romance and publish both novels in the one book hence the heading using the word, *Tales*.

We're on the starting blocks

Now we're getting close to writing the first draft of our novel to be completed in 8 weeks. But first we need the plot. Of course, if you are going to fly by the seat of your pants, you won't have a plot, although I reckon it can't hurt to study this chapter. You may even learn something worthwhile, and you can always return to your no-plot method later.

Before we start to plot, a family tree is a great idea. I always start a separate file containing the names of the characters. Without that list to hand, you can be writing your plot and draw a blank. What is the name of that character who bumps into Enrico at the market?

By placing the names on a sort of family tree, you have a list of character names and an overall view of how, if at all, they connect to one another. This is not a *description* of your characters, whether they are 2D or 3D, goodies or baddies, etc., but a list in diagram form. It's a great idea, a sort-of Elevator Pitch of your characters. Here's a family tree of the characters in my novel *All Their Christmases*. The characters are divided into family, employment, friends and sub-plot.

The family tree of the characters in *All Their Christmases*

Family
ENRICO (main character)
ROSIE (Main character)
Buster (Rosie's dog)

SOFIA (Enrico's older sister)

MARIA (Enrico's niece) MALCOLM/ANNA (Rosie's son/daughter-in-law)

JOSEPH & MICHAEL (Enrico's great nephews) PIP (Rosie's Granddaughter)

Employment
MIRANDA (Enrico and Rosie's Boss)
BIG GRAEME (Santa 2) LORNA (Mrs Santa 2) RUSSELL (Photographer)

Friends
BEVERLEY (Enrico's neighbour) ALFRID (Enrico's friend)

Sub-Plot
THOMAS (Divorced father) STEPHANIE (Divorced mother)
TIMMY (Young son of Thomas and Stephanie)

CHRISTINE
(Friend of Stephanie)

Having your characters in some graphic form makes it easy to see your story at a glance. You don't have to be a graphic artist to come up with a diagram such as the one on the previous page. Use what works for you.

How many characters?

Because we're writing a novel of between 40,000 and 50,000 words, there won't be a huge number of characters. One or two main characters is good. And once you've created your wall sign and elevator pitch, your family tree with its characters should be straightforward.

Now the family tree tells us the names and relationships, but not the personality, the character of the characters.

Having written your elevator pitch, you will know the broad outline of your story. You will know which characters are kind and loving, the one or ones who are greedy or nasty, and the one or ones who perhaps are going to get their comeuppance. Finally, there are the minor characters. These are usually human, but don't have to be, (Rosie's pal is her dog Buster), and are like ships that pass in the night. They can be described as the film extras in your novel. They need to be there but are not as important as the main characters. On the previous page, Beverley and Alfrid are needed but are minor characters.

So, with your title or working title, genre, elevator pitch, wall sign and list of characters in place, you're now ready to plot. On your marks!

Romance

For

Seniors

Chapter 4
Write your Plot

THERE ARE SEVERAL ways to plot, different methods of plotting. You choose the one that best suits you. Remember the better you plot, the better your first draft and the better your first draft, the better the final version of your novel.

Get the foundation (the plot) as detailed and as clearly set out as possible, and you will thank yourself as the words flow as you pen your first draft.

Here are three possible methods or ways to plot.

1. Chronological
2. Stream of Consciousness
3. The Three-Part Version

Just like your first draft, your plot is not set in stone. I think it should contain as much detail as possible and is subject to change. Be prepared to add and subtract. Once I start writing a novel, I get new ideas from time to time. I add them to the plot.

Your plot is your guide. It's the architect's drawing and you're the builder. Brilliant, fulsome plots allow you to write a first draft with speed and speed is the essence of success in this course. Get that first draft down on paper asap. Okay, let's plot.

#1 Chronological plotting

In this type of plot, you list the events in your novel as they occur over a passage of time. Chronological plotting requires a calendar. Think of it as a diary. What happened today? Tonight? Tomorrow? Again, because we're creating a short novel, your story won't cover centuries. Between 40 and 50 thousand words calls for a short period of time.

Your novel could cover as little as hours or days or a week or weeks.

So, you've chosen your genre, written your elevator pitch, made a list of characters, and your wall sign is sitting beside you on your desk or on your wall above your head. Now it's time to write that plot.

Does a chronological plot go in a straight line? Yes and no. If you want to write about an incident in the past, a flashback, then you put the appropriate date and add the plot details of when such and such happened. To keep the reader in the loop, you may need to add a date at the top of the page. Here's an example from my novel, *A Plum Jam*.

Lyon, France 1941

Louise Beatrice Wellesley, known at various times as Sister Claudine or Plum, walked away from Lyon. The bishop in the magnificent cathedral had just tried to murder her. She escaped after the religious toppled from the cathedral's balcony smashing onto a solid oak pew, decorating it and the floor with his blood, brains, and crucifix. Pity the cleaner involved with that lot.

I repeat, both your plot and first draft can be changed. Both should be written at a rapid rate without editing. Once your plot is finished, be ready to go back over it, removing or adding information. When the plot is ready, get stuck into your first draft.

Write at a rapid rate and only edit your first draft when it is finished. I'll repeat that previous sentence because it's super important.

Write at a rapid rate and **only edit your first draft when it is finished.**

Of course, any new ideas are added to your plot and thus to your first draft. But editing occurs **after** the first draft is finished. Throw away your rear-view mirror. When writing a first draft you do not look backwards.

Here's a chronological plot I used for my novel *All Their Christmases*. The story began on November 20 and finished soon after Christmas, a time span of about five weeks.

Nov 20
Meet Enrico, the first main character, and his relationship with older sister Sophia
She mothers her younger brother, a confirmed bachelor
He explains how he'll be performing as Santa again this year
He recalls with affection being contacted by Miranda, CEO of *Costumes 4 U*
Sonia worries he's too old and has a troublesome hip
Enrico sets off to shop. He features in a "Save the Cat" moment when he buys an ice-cream for an upset small child

Nov 21
We meet the other main character, Rosie, who has a special relationship with her only grandchild, the teenage Phillipa known as Pip
The women have a meal on Thursday night at Grannie's when Pip's parents are away
Dad (Rosie's son) is a long-distance lorry driver and Mum, (Rosie's daughter-in-law) is a women's hairdresser with late closing on Thursdays
Rosie tells Pip she is auditioning for a role as Mrs Santa in the local shopping centre
She wants the money to pay for an ocean cruise

Nov 25
The people keen to be Santa or Mrs Santa gather at *Costumes 4 U*
Big Graeme is big, crude and, like Enrico, an old hand at being Santa

Graeme and Enrico will work together, sharing shifts at the same shopping centre
The two Mrs Santa ladies, who will be their partners, are introduced
Lorna, a snob, was once a professional actress and is now a frustrated prima donna
Rosie works with costumes in amateur theatre and is friendly and kind
Enrico, the retired barber, offers his services for any adjustments to the ladies' coiffures
Big Graeme is loud and crude although charming when performing
Both couples could not be more different
Later that day, both Rosie and Enrico's family want to know what happened
Sofia worries "baby" brother might be taken advantage of by some scheming Mrs Santa
Pip wants to know all about Santa. Rosie likes Enrico and finds it tricky to tell the truth

Nov 28
It's a Sunday. Lunch at Sofia's where we meet Maria and her sons, Michael and Joseph
They are flash 20 somethings and call their great uncle Enrico, Ric
He reckons they are not respectful to him and especially not to women
A joke is made about Enrico getting married at Christmas where he has a Mrs Santa as a partner
The great nephews tease him and ask, "Is she hot, Ric?"
That afternoon he takes the train to the shopping centre for a trial run
He checks out the Santa set then sits for a coffee
Rosie appears having the same idea. He buys her a coffee and they chat
Their friendship develops. He explains the performing routine and dressing-room set-up
She offers to drive him home
He reluctantly agrees but gets out at the end of his street not wanting his address revealed
She drives off and both find their initial feelings of affection grow stronger

....

The plot continues with the relationship hitting hurdles. This is the important component of conflict in the story. Every story demands conflict. Will the budding romance amount to anything? Will it succeed? The month of December is when the couple perform as Santa and Mrs Santa with the climax of the novel happening on Christmas Eve.

All Their Christmases is a romance with a sub-plot. This involves a young married couple and their son. This family has no connection to the two main characters, Enrico and Rosie. It's good if you have a sub-plot or plots (I recommend only one to keep your novel short) which are unrelated to the main story. It keeps the reader guessing. What do these other characters have to do with the main plot? WARNING. Spoiler alert with plot details below.

In *All Their Christmases*, the young son of the couple, now divorced, becomes the focal point as he is kidnapped by his desperate father in the shopping centre where Enrico and Rosie are Mr and Mrs Santa. It's dramatic where luck, common sense and love triumphs.

Here we bring the main plot and the sub-plot together. Your plotting is good when unrelated plots become related. Readers like to see unresolved matters resolved. Avoid loose ends. You make that happen when you plot well.

#2 Stream of Consciousness Plotting

There are novels written using this method. I recommend it as a way of plotting your novel. Let the ideas flow and not necessarily in any order.

Stream of consciousness in a narrative is when the narrator, the writer, expresses all manner of thoughts and ideas without necessarily using any structure. You simply let the details flow. These details may not be connected but because they exist in the writer's brain, they are notated "as they come" so to speak.

So how would this work as a method of plotting your novel? I suggest in two ways as this is how I have used it. Not to write a novel but to plot.

First you notate any thought you have regarding your theme, characters, action, settings, events, even dialogue, etc, and second, you go back over what you've notated and assemble the pieces of the jigsaw placing them in a conventional plot scenario such as the previous one, the chronological plot.

I find it works by handwriting rather than typing my thoughts. I include lines of dialogue. The characters have firmed up. I know what they might say. My ideas will not necessarily be in order and parts may be discarded when I come to writing the novel. But this is a case where "less is more" is not true. More is better.

Have you ever tried brainstorming? This activity can work well when a group of people keen to solve a problem or build a strategy, gather and fire off ideas willy-nilly. You need someone to notate the suggestions. It often happens that one person's idea triggers another idea from someone else. What you're doing with a Stream of Consciousness plot, is brainstorming by yourself. Here's how it could work with *All Their Christmases*. My choice is to hand write the ideas. Here they are.

Enrico retired 71 bachelor lives alone happy in himself
Grows great veg his father was a greengrocer
Has inherited his parents' home not a mansion but a big block in outer eastern suburb and ideal
as a knock down and site for three or four townhouses
Strong relationship with older sister who mothers him
He accepts her fussy attention but at same time complains and gently pushes her away
His body is slowly aging his doctor tells him a hip replacement is just around the corner
He walks with a stick but tries to pretend he doesn't need it

When he feels strong, he puts stick on his shoulder to show the world, he's fit and healthy
Started work with his father in the fruit and veg business but got the chance to work with his
uncle who was a barber
He started by sweeping the floor became good at cutting hair for boys and men
About 30 he got the chance to hire a shop near home and spent 40 years as the local barber
Men who were boys when he cut their hair called in to say g'day
He retired when his parents died and now owns and lives alone in the house
Had a girlfriend when young but she dumped him, and he never got over it
Doesn't like his great nephews reckons they're selfish and treat women badly
In recent years he applied to become Santa in a local shopping centre
In his third year in the job at which he is brilliant the company running the show decide to have a
woman as well enter Mrs Santa
Here he meets Rosie, and they are attracted to one another
He is too shy to make any sort of romantic approach, and she is a lady and would never push
herself on anyone even someone she admires, likes and eventually falls in love with
The couple do fall for one another
It will be Rosie's second marriage and Enrico's first
He has no idea how to woo her and asks a mate, another Italian who is up to wife number 4
although the current partner is a common-law wife
The mate can't get over Enrico's naivete as the former barber asks basic love-making questions
Rosie's family are worried she is doing the Mrs Santa work so she can go on a cruise and with
single women possibly being a target and things like Covid ever present, they don't want her to
take the Mrs Santa job
When the romance begins, sister Sofia panics thinking some gold-digger woman is going to fleece
her little brother
That's just the half of it when the great nephews, Joseph and Michael, discover great uncle Enrico
may get hitched in his old age
They are the beneficiaries of his house, and any new wife might delay their windfall by years,
decades
They plan ways to disrupt the possible wedding and will fight dirty
Their big mistake is to wrongly identify Mrs Santa and think Lorna the bitter ex professional actor
is Ric's lover
Mistaken identity dominates
In a separate issue, a young married couple have a son, but the marriage turns sour
The wife's girlfriend piles in and encourages the young mother to divorce, and they engage a
lawyer to stitch up the husband
He's in danger of losing everything, his house, marriage and particularly his son and then his mind
He's so depressed he contemplates suicide, he's a walking time bomb
Need to bring the two plots together at the end

#3 The Three-Part Plot

This is where you divide your plot into three parts: a beginning, a middle and an end. Almost all novels can be divided like so. When plotting, you concentrate on one section at a time. Get each section right, string them together and you've created your plot.

Then write your first draft following your Three-Part Plot. Let's consider the three parts.

The beginning

1. Your first sentence
2. Establish your genre
3. Introduce your protagonist (and possibly your antagonist)

It should be obvious that your first sentence must grab the reader's attention. But remember this is the plot not the first draft. You can tinker with your first sentence after you finish the first draft. Just get your first sentence down knowing it should make the reader curious and lead them to ask questions.

It's essential to establish your genre in the beginning, help the reader discover your novel really is a mystery, romance, fantasy or whatever. How? Look at the beginning of novels in the same genre. What do they contain which establishes their genre?

Mind you, your blurb on the back cover (or early on in an eBook) is another way to announce your genre.

And of course you should, rather *must* introduce your protagonist. Who is he or she? What do they want to achieve? What are the problems they face, the obstacles they need to overcome? Is the antagonist blocking their journey? In the beginning section of your plot, you establish the basics of your novel.

The middle

This is usually the largest part of your novel and can be tricky for some (or is that all?) novelists. Look at it as the bridge between the opening and closing of your tale. You've started the race, and you know there's a finish line on the horizon but to get to the end, you must cross the bridge. This is where you build on the core of your novel, may introduce a sub-plot and start building towards the climax.

Good plotting will see you ask, "Am I building the tension in the middle section?" I like the expression "ramping up the tension".

Stand back and look at your plot points. Is the protagonist suffering? Is he/she under increasing pressure? If not, what can I do to add to their problems? How can I ramp up the danger, the possible pain the protagonist may or will suffer?

Ask yourself, "Am I getting bogged down?" The middle section can have what is known as a saggy bottom. You must maintain activity. This doesn't have to be gunfire and car chases – it could be – but you must keep moving. Too much description can be a drag. Likewise unnecessary dialogue. Pacing is what keeps the reader interested.

The end

Every section of your novel has potential booby traps but the end particularly so. Let's be positive and point to what you should do.

Resolve every issue and especially the protagonist's main problem/goal. It can be annoying even infuriating for a reader to reach the end of a novel and not know what happened to so and so or leave the conflict up in the air. We want to know what happened.

There's nothing wrong with having a cliffhanger at the end particularly if your novel is part of a series. This can be the hook to have the reader seek out the next book in the series. But be careful if the novel is not part of a series, what is called a standalone novel, and your cliffhanger is never resolved. Your readers are your most important partners. Treat them well with respect; some would add love. Avoid being too clever by half.

How have your main characters changed? They've been on a journey. Have you clearly shown what your protagonist's life has become?

Where is the best place for your climax? You've been building the tension from the beginning and especially in the middle. You will be guided by the amount of time you need to spend on winding down, even explaining what happened after the climax.

If you are planning on affirming that justice should be done and even be seen to be done, you need to make this clear as part of the end of your novel.

Unresolved or unexpected endings. If you leave some part of the story incomplete, different readers may react in varying ways. You don't want them throwing your novel at the wall. A twist in the tail/tale can be effective or upsetting. What matters is that you are pleased with what your plot contains. Once that is done, grab your quill and start writing that first draft. Flat out.

Warning. Be wary of introducing anything new in your end section. New characters, a new sub-plot are not needed and will get in the way of your fabulous finish.

Mix Your Plots

You could write your plot using the Three-Part Plot as the frame, but then setting out the details using the Chronological Plot. Or some other combination. And you can search for "plotting a novel" methods and discover more than the three listed here. The right method is the one you like, the one that works for you.

Remember the stronger, the more detailed your plot, the more you will know about your characters and the events in your novel. This means your task of writing your first draft is made … I nearly wrote *easier* then and we know writing is never easy. A solid and detailed plot helps your writing flow even blossom when you tackle your first draft.

The opposite is true. You could make your plot light, devoid of much detail and that might cause you to stop penning your first draft as you scramble to make your first draft sing. To make the words of your first draft flow, stuff your plot with anything, anything to do with your characters, events and conflict.

"The main plot line is simple: getting your character to the foot of the tree, getting him up the tree, and then figuring out how to get him down again."
Jane Yolen

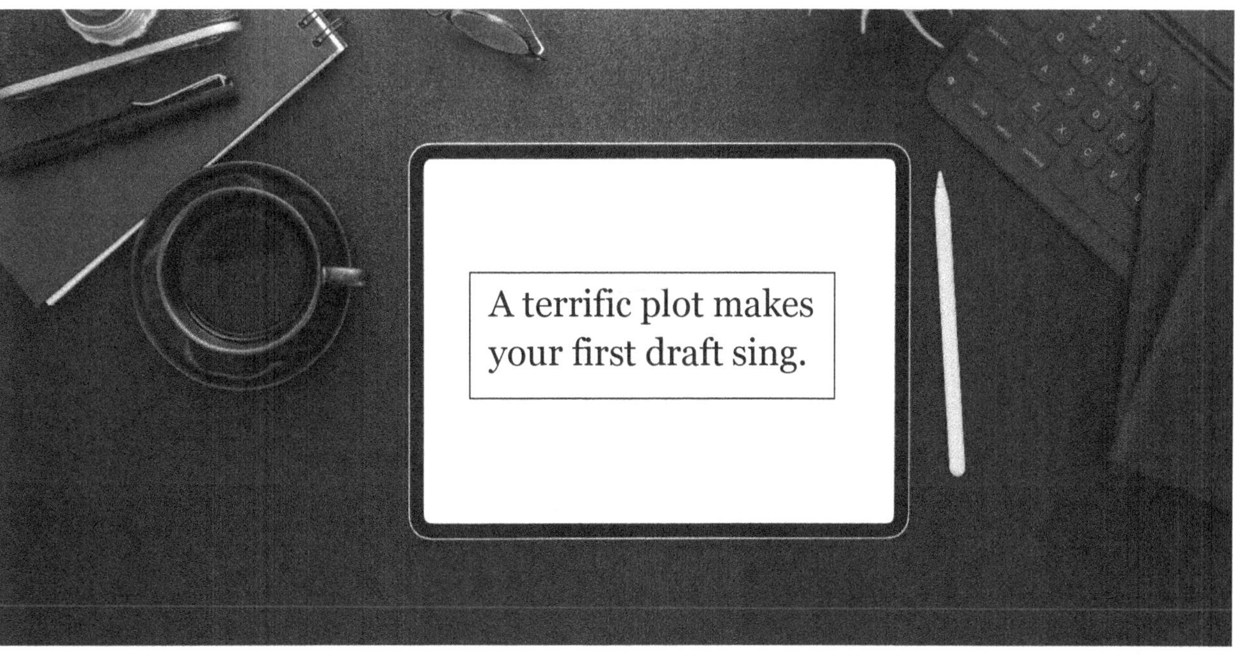

Chapter 5
Plot in Half a Day

NOW WE START. Here's a check list.

- ✓ Genre chosen
- ✓ Elevator pitch written
- ✓ Wall sign in place
- ✓ List of characters – at least their names
- ✓ Title selected
- ✓ Plot method chosen

With those six things established, give yourself three hours (or less if you're enthusiastic) and write your plot. The best advice I can give is to embrace speed. Sitting there pondering what comes next won't buy the child a frock. Fast plotting is good plotting.

As previously mentioned, I like to choose the title from the off. Even if it's a working title, choose early. You don't want to be working on "that novel" or "my novel". Give it a name.

How to write between 40,000 and 50,000 words?

It's all in your plot.

- ✓ Limit number of characters
- ✓ Limit time span of story
- ✓ Limit sub-plots

One or two main characters and a few minor characters is fine.
Your story takes place over days, weeks or perhaps a month or two.
One sub-plot is more than enough.

If you have your sub-plot disconnected from your main story, and only bring the two together at the end – that's clever plotting – you will have done well.

I wish you good luck and will resume contact once you've finished your plot.

Chapter 6
Write Your First Draft

I'M ASSUMING CONGRATULATIONS are in order, and your plot is finished. Well done you. So, with your plot by your side or on your screen, you switch between plot and first draft with a keyboard shortcut if you're typing and create the first draft of your novel. Here are some important tips.

Stay well. This is a tough ask especially if you're new to novel writing. Not getting enough sleep or eating badly will hinder your progress.

Aim for the **same time and place** in which to write. It's not a deal-breaker but good habits can help you complete your first draft on time.

Be organized. Even if you have an untidy desk/writing area, give yourself the benefit of being able to find anything essential in a nanosecond. Okay, two nanoseconds.

Remove distractions. Some writers enjoy hearing music as they write. Having a cat on your lap might be calming for you and the cat but remove unnecessary distractions. The aim is to set yourself up in a situation which helps not hinders the flow of your words.

The point about being able to **back-up your work** needs to be shouted from the rooftops. You may have software that automatically saves your work every few minutes. MS Word has an Auto Recover tab where you nominate the time your work is to be saved e.g. every ten minutes.

At the end of the day, I send the file of my work to myself as an attachment in an email. In the unlikely event of your hard drive and USB stick exploding or being stolen, it's another way to back up your work. Your Internet Service Provider (ISP) should have your emails on tap.

I keep a daily record of my **word count**. This is helpful when wanting/needing to average a certain number of words a day. It can be a source of encouragement. 'Wow! Look what I've done today!' And if it reveals you've slipped behind your minimum daily output, it can be a whip with which to give you a flick to lift your game.

I list the number of words when I stop work during any 24-hour period by placing a single line (|) after the figure and placing a double line (||) when I finish for the day.

642 | 1163 || 1989 || 2701 || 3510 | 3818 || etc

On Day 1 over two sessions I wrote 1163 words. On Day 2 over one session I wrote 826 words. On Day 3 I wrote 712 words, and on Day 4 over two sessions I wrote 1117 words. Keeping a record helps.

Consistency is a powerful tool. If you are writing 200 words one day and 2,000 words the next, you are not being consistent. You might argue, 'Yes, but my average word count is 1,100 words.' True but creating a routine gets your mind and your body clock, whatever that is, in a groove. You need to write around eight hundred words a day and by being consistent, may soon find you do!

I'll see you on the other side

This *Write a Novel in Eight Weeks* course contains sections on improving your writing, editing, self-publishing, and launching and marketing your novel.

In Improving your Writing section, we examine aspects such as the POV, Show Don't Tell, Save the Cat, Change Passive to Active, Unnecessary Words, Kill Your Darlings and more.

If we launch into those things now, you will cruel your chances of finishing your first draft in eight weeks or less. Remember you are most welcome to finish ahead of time.

You may argue you are using this book to make your writing better. And I hope and plan to make sure you do. But the focus of this book is to **finish** your novel and **publish** it.

Once you complete your first draft, all those writing tips we examine can be applied as you edit your work. Remember that all-important rule in writing your first draft. Do not look back or rather, only look forward. Write without stopping. Okay, sleeping and eating are allowed.

So right now, dear writer, I am going to pick up my swag and head off into the bush. When I return, you will have finished your first draft. Yes, <u>finished</u> your first draft. That is the sole aim, the core, the basis, and the raison d'être of this course.

And to prevent you taking a sneak peek at the writing and self-publishing tips which follow, I have thrown in a blank page or two. Yes, of course, it is a waste of paper, but it is an attempt to emphasize your sole immediate task.

Do nothing but write your first draft. Fast.

I will see you on the other side.

Break a leg!

You're writing your first draft.

Keep going.

Push on.

Chapter 7
Edit, Edit, Edit, Edit, Edit ...

CONGRATULATIONS. Completing your first draft is a mighty achievement. Doing so in 8 weeks or fewer is terrific. But now for the hard work. I mean the even harder hard work.

As mentioned before, a first draft is never perfect. In fact, it may well be terrible. But do not forget another fact; you cannot edit what doesn't exist.

A first draft is both the best and worst version of your novel. It's the best because it exists and is the worst because it will likely have all manner of issues – structural, spelling, punctuation, repetition, wrong and unnecessary words and more. Which is where the title of this chapter comes in. It's time to edit.

Should you edit your own writing?

Definitely. You will find many things you wish to change. You must edit your own work.

Should someone else edit your writing?

Definitely. They too may find many things they believe you should change.

Some people reckon you should never self-edit arguing you can't see the wood for the trees. I disagree. I repeat, I reckon every novelist should edit their own work. The real issue being should they then hand their work to a professional editor?

To help make that decision, the matter of money arises. Yes, you want the best possible version of your novel but if an editor charges hundreds, even thousands for their services, can you afford that? And how do you locate the ideal editor, and will they do a great job, whatever we mean by great? Finally, is there an alternative?

Yes, in the form of another novelist, a writing buddy. Someone with experience and editing knowledge is ideal, but a genuine and enthusiastic fellow writer should give excellent feedback. They are a new set of eyes to look at your novel.

The decisions about the editing of your novel are down to you. Consider the matters discussed in this chapter, talk to other writers who have used professional editing services, investigate what professionals offer and their fee, and then decide. I use fellow writers as editors on a quid pro quo basis sometimes called mutual back scratching.
Here are some good rules to start your editing.

Do nothing. Walk away. Now that advice seems to fly in the face of the book's title. Time is short and we only have three weeks (it could be more if you wrote your first draft quickly) to edit and publish the novel.

By walk away I mean give yourself a break. Not for a week but certainly for at least 24 hours. If you've been slaving over a hot keyboard for 50 odd days, it's good to give yourself a break. If you are writing say a 75,000-word novel over several months, once you finish your first draft, I would recommend you steer clear of anything to do with the novel for at least a week. Give yourself a serious break.

Use a spellcheck. Most software programmes will highlight spelling and punctuation mistakes. I click on them and follow their advice knowing there is much more "hands on" editing to do.

AI is getting better but spellcheck can fail with say homonyms. You write, 'I applied the car's breaks.' That gets a tick of approval from the spell checker when in fact you should have written, 'I applied the car's brakes.'

Read your tome in one go. Having used a spell checker for the whole first draft, I like to read the novel in one setting. You could read it silently or aloud, or you could have it read to you. I like listening to someone read my novel to me. As a Word file or its Mac equivalent, or if you convert your document to a PDF, there are simple steps to have it read from cover to cover.

With the PDF version of your novel in front of you, click on the **A))** icon at the top of the screen and then the **Voice Option** link at the top of the screen on the right. Here there's a drop-down menu where you can choose either a male or female voice and select an accent from a list of dozens of countries. Play around with different voices until you find the one you like.

A similar option is available with Microsoft Word. Under **Review**, is the <u>Read Aloud Speech</u> icon. I use both options.

As the narrator reads your novel, be prepared for some words to be mispronounced. This will happen if you have written unusual words or if the narrator you choose is from a country/region where the emphasis on syllables is not how you speak; *con*tribute and con*trib*ute is an example.

Again, we're back on the "only look forward" scenario. Just as you plot, and then write your first draft without stopping to edit, here I suggest you listen without stopping. I have a notepad (a paper one) and pen or pencil to hand and list a page number when I hear/see something I need to change or at least check.

As the mistake or query occurs, I write the page number and then a number representing the location. So, an error in the middle of page 4 would be written as 4.5. A mistake on the bottom of page 23 would be 23.9. It's an approximate location but it works well. Once the audio rendition ends, you go back to 11.1 or 18.7 or wherever and make your edit.

How About Your Pen Pal?

Previously I mentioned the international writing platform, NaNoWriMo. Have you explored this group? Have you joined it? Are you a member of a writing class in your area?

I mention all this because one of the best editing tools at your disposal could be another budding novelist. I've been lucky meeting two novelists online who have given me excellent advice as well as sending detailed suggestions for the entire novel.

One writer helped me with choice and size of font, spacing between lines and general layout when choosing a printer. Before that I'd been flying in the dark.

Finding the right writing partner/s is key. You help them and they help you. It's mutual. I've never paid for their editing expertise other than return the favour when one of their novels arrived awaiting my comments. I found the best way to benefit is to give generously of your time to others.

How do you find the ideal writing buddy?

Good question. By joining a writing course or book club or organization like NaNoWriMo means you have several lines in the water. I met people interested and active in novel writing on writing blogs. I would read the blog and then the readers' comments. I would make a comment. If someone wrote something I found interesting, I would reply and from such exchange of views, I found two writing buddies. To make a comment on the blog, you needed to add your name and email address.

Both my fellow novelists wrote in different genres which was never a problem. A well-written novel is a well-written novel regardless of genre.

Another benefit of editing each other's work is we can post a review of one another's writing. This shared experience has both artistic and marketing benefits.

Now having someone give you feedback on your novel doesn't mean you have to accept it. I study the comments in detail. Usually, I accept them but there are times when I don't. As a self-publisher, the editing buck stops with you.

Here's **a big No-no**. Do not send your novel for editing until you know you've done the best possible editing job you can do. You are wasting your time sending your writing buddy material which needs plenty of re-writing. Send them your best version.

There may be a few mistakes in your edited novel, but you are insulting your fellow novelist and wasting their time and yours asking them to comment on a work which has not been edited in detail. I would lose interest in working with someone who sent me unedited or poorly edited material.

Types of editing

Editing is not simply finding any missing commas and correcting spelling mistakes. Of course, such things are important, but editing can be described as a multi-layered operation. Here are some different types of editing provided by professionals.

- ✓ Developmental
- ✓ Line
- ✓ Copy
- ✓ Proof

A **developmental editor** looks at your novel from almost every direction. The characters and plot are studied. Is there tension when needed? Is the pace maintained? Do the characters stay in character and develop in an appropriate arc? What are the strengths and weaknesses of the work? An experienced developmental editor wants your voice to shine through and explains how it can be done.

A **line editor** studies your book a line or a sentence at a time. They look for consistency of voice, awkward sentences, unnecessary words, etc. They want to see the tone of your book improve. After a line editor has finished with your book, there should not be a wrong or unnecessary word to be seen.

A **copy editor** starts work when most of the other editing work is complete. They tackle the nuts and bolts of your novel – its grammar, punctuation and spelling, etc. They become the fact-checkers making sure that dates, places and events are spot on. The text the *Chicago Manual of Style* is the publishing bible. For example, it includes information of what word/s should be placed in italics. See line above where a book title appears.

A **proofread** edit happens at the end before you (or your printer) press the Print button. Has a line of text disappeared? Is there a missing word? Are the page numbers correct? Are the titles and chapter headings in place? This final edit aims to avoid a disaster.

I remember a commercial, pre-digital printer ringing me to say he'd spotted a typo in the opening paragraph of one of my novels he was about to print. Old-fashioned machinery was involved here where the printer, a human, put plates (paper or metal) on a drum, and then the printer, still the human, climbed on top of the two-metre-high machine to pour ink into the belly of the beast. Not like today with digital printing.

The printer and I managed to make a passable correction but that is an example of how proofreading is essential.

Today my novels are printed without plates from PDF files of the text and the cover by a machine which is a small fraction of the size of those older, gigantic units.

Widows and Orphans

Sometimes your text will spill over to the next page. Let's say three words appear. They'll look lonely all by themselves. They are your widows and orphans, an interchangeable term. Do you want to leave them there? You could have a whole line of text or two or three lines. If you don't want a mass of white space – not that white space is necessarily a bad thing – then you go back in that chapter and edit, you trim your text. It's official because a style manual suggests you "rewrite a portion of the paragraph" which will drag your widows and orphans from their position on the last page of the chapter, put them back with their family, and your last page of that chapter will disappear, reducing the number of pages in your novel.

Summary

- ✓ Editing is essential
- ✓ There are many professional services available
- ✓ There are different types of editing
- ✓ Self-editing as a starting point is essential
- ✓ There are many free editing options available
- ✓ The choice of hiring a professional editor is your call
- ✓ How is your writing buddy? They can be a great help.

"The secret to editing your work is simple: you need to become its reader instead of its writer." **Zadie Smith**

Chapter 8
Take a Breather

BEFORE WE CONTINUE, let's consider what we've covered, discovered so far.

- ✓ We defined the type of novel to be written in this course. It's a fictional story between 40,000 and 50,000 words, and we aim to finish the first draft in 8 weeks, although it could be sooner.

- ✓ We talked about the various methods of publishing including self-publishing.

- ✓ We discovered how to control the number of words in our novel to produce an amount between 40,000 and 50,000.

- ✓ Every novel is divided into three, usually unequal parts – the beginning, the middle and the end. That's unequal in size not in importance – each part is important, vital even.

- ✓ Many novels have three activities – the plot, the prose and the polish.

- ✓ We considered the difference between a plotter and a pantser.

- ✓ We did the maths – 40,000 words in 8 weeks equals about 700 words a day and 50,000 words in 8 weeks is about 900 words a day. These are average daily targets.

- ✓ We learnt about writing buddies down the street and half-way around the world.

- ✓ We discovered genre, elevator pitch and wall sign.

- ✓ We drew up a list of characters and how to do so using a form of family tree.

- ✓ And then we discovered there are many ways to plot a novel. We studied three.

- ✓ We wrote our plot.

- ✓ We wrote our first draft.

- ✓ We learnt about different types of editing.

- ✓ And now we're about to study ways to improve our writing.

Chapter 9
Improve Your Writing

AS YOU WORK through the topics in this chapter, you can return to your <u>finished</u>, your completed first draft and begin to edit using the information below. Remember speed is the name of the game. You can't edit what doesn't exist and you can't publish what hasn't been polished. Well, you can publish a novel which needs further editing but why would you do that? Best work only, please.

Character names

Look at your list. Are you happy with your choices? Choice is a personal matter, it's subjective. But the novelist, you, must feel comfortable with those names.

There was an English actress who didn't feel "in character" until she found the right footwear for her role. In her ideal shoes, slippers, boots or whatever, she was ready to go. I'm the same with names. You know your character and finding what you reckon is the perfect name, can only be good for your writing.

I like nicknames. I wrote a four-book series where the protagonist was christened Louise Beatrice Wellesley (distant relation of the 1st Duke of Wellington) but was known throughout as Plum. Her initials and cricket are involved. It should have been Plumb but that's another story. Having a history or background to your character, including their name, adds to their 3D nature. Create a history for your main character/s.

Here are some fictional names. Do you know them? More importantly, do you think they are appropriate? Robinson Crusoe, Elizabeth Bennet, Hieronymus Bosch, Atticus Finch.

In Len Deighton's political thriller, spy novel *The IPCRESS File*, the main character is an anti-hero. He's a soldier in the British Army serving overseas where he makes a quid on the black market. To avoid jail, he agrees to work for a secret branch of British Intelligence in London. He's a womanizer and despises those in authority. He's the protagonist in the novel so what would you call him?

(a) Humphrey Littleton-Jones (b) Jeremy Winstanley or (c) Harry Palmer?

It can be good to give your characters, particularly main characters, an appropriate name, one you enjoy and feel comfortable with. We're again playing with subjective here.

Len Deighton chose Harry Palmer.

Characters – 2D or 3D?

A two-dimensional character has height and width but no depth. A three-dimensional character has height, width and depth. Which is more interesting? Why?

A 2D character is usually insignificant and can be like a ship passing in the night. They exist but we don't know much, if anything, about them and importantly, we probably don't care about them. Characters in a pantomime on stage are always 2D.

However, a 3D character is important even massively so. If readers keep reading to (a) discover if a character changes or (b) because they care about a character, then 3D characters are the key to your novel's success.

They have a heart, a soul, a goal, a dream, a desire and more, and that's what makes them 3D. As a novelist, you must reveal (slowly perhaps) the inner workings of your 3D character making them a living person, someone the reader can care about, love, hate or despise. Mind you the timing of the reveal can be as important as the reveal itself.

List the characters in your novel and give each a mark - 2D or 3D.

Show Don't Tell

What does it mean? Anton Chekhov, a prominent Russian playwright and short story writer of the late 19th century, once said, "Don't tell me the moon is shining; show me the glint of light on broken glass." That quote captures the essence of Chekhov's writing style, which emphasizes the power of showing rather than telling.

Remember one definition of three parts of every novel, viz., DAD?
Description, Action, Dialogue.
Show Don't Tell is where ACTION trumps DESCRIPTION.

Examples
Description: Susie was frightened.
Action: Susie bit her lip, stifled a scream and dived under the blankets.

Now the example above defies the tip of *Make it stronger not longer*, as there are more words in the re-write. But look at the power change. All the action of lip biting, stifling a scream and diving (a good action word) under the blanket brings the description to life.

When you master *Show Don't Tell*, it is a win-win situation. You feel great because you have inserted colour, emotion, and reality to your story. The reader feels they are inside the character and wants to keep reading. Win win.

POV – Point of View

Novelists can write their novel in first, second or third person. You need to ask yourself the question, "Who is telling the story?" If it's a character in your story observing and describing what's happening, then your POV is First Person. It's usually your protagonist telling the tale, but it doesn't have to be. It could be another character.

If your storyteller is a narrator, not a character in your story, then your POV is Third Person. This is a common way of telling a story. There are two types of Third Person POV - third person omniscient and third person limited.

If the narrator has an omniscient POV, they can see and know everything. If they have a limited POV, third person limited, then they see everything only through one character's view. That character is usually the protagonist.

Second Person is uncommon and it's where the reader is addressed as *you*, being addressed directly. It's akin to live theatre where the actor steps through the fourth wall and speaks directly to the audience. The fourth wall is the invisible space through which the audience watches the play and behind which the actors perform.

The two important keys re POV are (a) choose the one you feel happiest with using and (b) never mix 'n match. If someone is reading your novel which starts in the Third Person and then to keep telling the story you, the novelist, switches to the First Person, confusion reigns supreme. Choose one POV and stick with it.

What to do with Ideas?

Ideas for a novelist are what makes the world go round. They are essential, the food we need. They can arrive at any time. You could be lying in bed, standing under the shower, sitting in a cinema watching a film or driving a car.

I don't know where ideas come from or what triggers their arrival in my head. I remember a movie director being interviewed. I agree with his answer.

Interviewer: Where do you get your ideas from?
Movie director: I think of them.

I suggest you ignore how and where they come from but get stuck into notating them. Failing to immediately notate can be a fatal mistake. You wake up and have an idea, something to do with your current project, something you never considered pops into your head, and it sounds perfect or at least interesting. Not all ideas work. As it is 2.30 am, you roll over making a mental note to record the idea in the morning.

Wrong! You wake up hours later and can't for the life of you remember that idea. You torture yourself trying to remember even a keyword of your nocturnal lightbulb moment. Nothing. You've lost what could have been a terrific addition to your novel.

So, here's the preparation to ensure such a situation never happens to you.

Always have a pen/pencil and paper handy. Don't make a note in the dark. Bad handwriting is bad enough, but notating blind can be a disaster. An alternative to pen and paper is your phone. You could use it to notate your ideas.

But if notating ideas is essential, so too is filing them. Whether you work digitally or by handwriting or speaking into a recording device, you must be organized. Have a solid filing system and a back-up. A successful novelist is an organized novelist.

Writing Dialogue

The spoken words in your novel can be called direct speech or dialogue. In a play, almost all the words in the playscript, are dialogue. Remember a novel is divided into three sections as the Beginning, Middle and End and as DAD – Description, Action and **Dialogue.** Here are some rules for writing the spoken words, the dialogue.

You have a choice with punctuation. You can use double quotation marks, "spoken words," or single quotation marks, 'spoken words.'

Publishers in different countries use different versions. As a self-publisher, you can please yourself. I use single quotation marks. American English features "double quotation marks," whereas British English uses 'single quotation marks.'

As small as it may be, single quotation marks take up less space. You might think it a minor matter but over many pages, it can mount up and even reduce the number of pages in your novel. Fewer pages equals a cheaper cost of printing.

Dialogue rules

A new speech appears on a new line although a character making two speeches with a description between speeches doesn't require a new line. Whenever a new speaker's speech appears, you must start a separate line. Even if the speech is one word, the following speech must begin on a new, a separate line.

Unless it's obvious who is speaking, you must identify the speaker. Example.

'Katerina is late,' said Jess.

If only two characters are in the scene, no ID is needed after the first two speeches. Example.

> 'Fred is late,' said Dot.
> 'He's always late,' said Brian.
> 'I'll murder him if he's forgotten the cake.'
> 'I'll murder him anyway.'

In the example above, Dot spoke and then Brian spoke. They are the only two characters in the scene. With a separate line for each new speech, we can correctly assume, each character follows the other. From line 3 onwards, we don't need *said Dot* or *said Brian*.

Exercise

Write four lines of dialogue involving two characters.

Must it always be "said"?

Writing teachers differ on this point. Some say using *said* to identify the characters can get boring. You finish up with many repetitions.

> 'I thought we were going to attack at dawn,' said Pierre.
> 'It's been postponed for 24 hours,' said Gabrielle.
> 'But the forecast for Tuesday is horrible,' said Danny.

Others reckon the word *said* is not important. Of course, you need it to identify the speaker but what *is* important is the choice of words, the way they are spoken and to whom. Supporters of *said* say, 'Go with *said*.'

Another opinion is you swap *said* for such words as *whispered*, *yelled* or *begged*. But then if you replaced *said* with one or more of those descriptive words, the scene could become overwhelming, crammed with *screamed, mumbled* and *hissed*.

And this point demonstrates how so many writing situations are subject to different opinions bringing the word *subjective* yet again to the fore.

Save the Cat

This was originally an idea invented by the American, Blake Snyder, for screenplay writers. There is now a method of plotting your screenplay or novel called *Save the Cat*.

The basic principle involves creating a scene designed to make the reader like or feel good about a certain character. He or she is walking in the street, sees a house on fire with a cat trapped at an upstairs window. The character rescues the animal and thus gains favour in the eyes of your reader or audience. Someone saved the cat.

Usually, you insert this activity towards the beginning of your story, so we establish the nature of the character early on. In my novel *All Their Christmases*, I wanted to demonstrate how the 71-year-old protagonist, Enrico, was all heart, one of the good guys.

He approached the store when a young mother came out with a pushchair. She was Ms Fecund having a 3-year-old holding Mum's free hand, the one not controlling the baby conveyance. Its rear was packed with groceries because in the front was infant number two.

The sight impressed Enrico; two under three must be a handful. But no, the roll call was incomplete. Across Mum's chest in a sling or papoose-like device lay a sleeping new-born—*three* kids! That's a lotta nappies!

Enrico slowed to admire the convoy. How long did the mother take to prepare her brood for a trip to the outside world?

The walking child adored licking an ice-cream in a cone when disaster struck. Her enthusiastic tongue proved too strong, and the scoop of the yummy cold stuff climbed out of the cone, proved the theory of gravity to be true, and took a kamikaze dive splattering face down on the footpath.

The little girl's wail saw heads turn and concerned citizens move to see if help was required. Enrico had a front-row seat. No bones broken, no fingers squeezed, but 98% of her prized ice-cream stuck to the footworn asphalt. Mind you it was swept clean every morning.

Two pigeons waddled in keen to strike. The early bird gets the churn.

The retired barber disappeared as Mum tried to pacify the mortified offspring. Her siblings, including the one asleep, came out in sympathy and soon the neighbourhood discovered their representative in this year's Best Bawling Babies bash.

Of course, motherhood has always been a soda. All this current Mum need do was pacify all three without dropping the newborn, keep the groceries aboard the vehicle, and set off for home. As stated, a soda.

About to depart, the upset family stopped because Enrico blocked their path. This became the final straw for the exasperated mother.

Enrico bent from the waist, a major achievement, and smiled at the oldest of the crying trio. From behind his back appeared another ice-cream, this time a frozen confection on a stick.

The crying stopped in a nanosecond. As if by magic, the siblings followed big sis with the one in the push chair thinking, *Anyfing f'me?*

The knight in shining armour offered the confection to the child. Her dumbfounded mother spoke.

'What do you say, Lily?'

The child knew the routine, said 'Thank you,' and accepted the gift. Her eyes sparkled and her tongue tackled a new task.

'Thank you, kind sir,' said Mum. She fumbled for her purse. 'Let me pay you.'

'Don't be silly,' said Enrico. 'You deserve it doing a brilliant job with such a fine-looking family.'

The woman smiled, looked massively relieved and set off but stopped, turned back and spoke with a soft voice.

'You would make a wonderful Father Christmas.'

She and her kids departed with the former barber grinning inside and out.

The passage above is an example of *Save the Cat* where an action by a character shows them to be a good person, someone kind who most readers are likely to like or admire.

Change Passive to Active

Writing in general and novel writing in particular is full of rules and new writers may become so keen to follow them, they find themselves in a mess. One approach is to ignore rules as you write your first draft. Write the words and, when you have finished your first draft, think about the rules in your editing stage.

Further to that, I have never found a writing rule which says you cannot write in the passive voice.

Passive   Keith was killed by the burglar.
Active   The burglar killed Keith.

Here are a couple of thoughts on active and passive voice. If you continually write in the passive voice, it may prompt readers to close your book and read something else.

You can have active verbs and thus write in the active voice but still write a dull sentence. *Show Don't Tell* could creep in here.

Shunning passive voice can sometimes be impossible. If you are telling a tale in which a victim is involved, speaking from the victim's POV is well served using passive voice.

One question you can ask during your editing stage is, does my sentence, passive or active, leave no stone unturned? If you write, *The police officer struck the prisoner* or *The prisoner was struck by the police officer,* neither tells us the whole story. Was it a deliberate blow? Was it self-defence? Who started the action and why? Can the action be justified from a legal or moral POV?

Unnecessary Words

Books about writing may include a list of words you should use sparingly if at all. Again, this is advice you can take or leave. When editing, I will do a search for these words and have often found they can be deleted without changing the meaning of the sentence. Why these words?

Well, as the title of the section states, they are unnecessary. Why *suddenly* is usually unnecessary. By using *suddenly,* you are removing the shock a sudden event can have on the reader. You are warning the reader that something is about to happen. It's a sort of spoiler alert.

The words *almost* and *quite* are friends. They attach themselves to verbs as adverbs and we know Stephen King says, 'remove all adverbs.'

Never say never but avoid these words where possible.

suddenly
that
had
almost
then
started to/began to

NOT It started to rain – **INSTEAD** It's raining

Implied words
NOT She nodded her head. (What else is she going to nod?) **USE** She nodded.

just, really, very, perhaps/maybe
quite, amazing, literally, stuff, things, got, some
look, get, noticed, was, felt

Kill Your Darlings

There's a movie, a biographical drama with this name. In writing circles, the saying is sometimes referred to as kill *my* darlings. It's advice suggesting you should cut a word or words, even a character, from your book. Why? Because they are unnecessary, they don't add anything to your story, they don't reveal something important about a character or move the action. They can be removed without trace and doing so will improve your work.

The word *darlings* refers to the fact you have slaved over a hot keyboard to create this material, and you love your work. It can be a kick in the guts to learn your much-loved prose, your darlings, are for the chop. It's called needs must. The quality of your tome tops everything.

I wrote a musical called *Toys*. After weeks of rehearsals and close to opening night, someone took me aside and pointed out that one of the nine characters in the show was unnecessary, redundant. You could assign that character's lines to other characters and the show would work as well if not better. They were right. I had written an unnecessary character. For subsequent seasons, the script was changed.

Your First Sentence and First Paragraph

Some people pick up a book and start reading. At the end of the first sentence, some will have seen enough and replace said tome. Some will become interested and read to the end of the first paragraph, and some will reckon this book's a bit of all right and reach for their wallet. That tells you something about the importance of your first sentence and first paragraph. Spend time on both.

First sentence

As an exercise, hand write your first sentence. I find handwriting concentrates the mind more than when typing. Now re-write your first sentence three more times.

Tackle it from another angle. Don't simply use synonyms to re-write, turn the sentence upside down, come at it as if you're creating it for the first time. Here's an example.

ORIGINAL: Michelle grinned, reached for the knife and loved the look on his face.
RE-WRITE 1: The burglar shat himself as the smiling homeowner crept towards him.
RE-WRITE 2: As the dribbling woman raised the sharpened knife it glinted.
RE-WRITE 3: Break and enter has its downsides.

The aim is to make your first sentence a killer diller from Manilla, i.e. outstanding. Look at your variations and go for the one you reckon is the best.

First Paragraph

Here are some ideas, some ways to create a brilliant first paragraph. Pick a theme.

- ✓ Mystery
- ✓ Danger
- ✓ Character
- ✓ Action
- ✓ Dramatic ending

The following examples are from novels I've written. Here's an example using **mystery** in your first paragraph.

"What a mess. Sherlock Holmes was rarely tidy, and right now his sitting-room had lost all self-respect. The great detective didn't care. He was soon to retire, off to Sussex and a new life as an apiarist. Meet beekeeper Holmes."
Cenarth Fox, *Sherlock Holmes: Playing the Game*

Now an example using **danger** in your first paragraph.

"You can be sacked from almost any job. You can be ignored, bullied and demoted but there aren't many jobs where you can be tortured, raped and murdered.
Cenarth Fox, *A Plum Job*

Now let's say you want to reveal a character's **character** in your first paragraph.

"I was always first. It was in my genes. My parent's chromosomes had an abundance of punctuality cells. I can't help myself being early and occasionally, no, pretty much never, I'm on time." **Cenarth Fox,** *Barnum Misquoted*

Here's an example putting **action** into your first paragraph.

The gun appeared in the open doorway. The woman in the kitchen flicked through a Vogue lift-out, angry at the faces of so many wrinkle-free females. At 63, Sheila's skin clearly belonged in the before section of the before-and-after ads for women of a certain age. Botox be my friend. **Cenarth Fox,** *Tricky Conscience*

Finally, study this example of ending your first paragraph with **a bang.**

"He yelled, she screamed and the violent domestic kicked off. Passengers scattered. The Clifton Hill Up platform was packed and a scratching, slapping, shrieking barney got people moving. Did it ever." **Cenarth Fox,** *The Code of Monte Christo*

You want your editing to include every jot and tittle of your text, but your first sentence and your first paragraph can be the difference between your book being bought or left alone and unloved.

Chapter 10
The Look of Your Book

ONCE YOUR NOVEL has been edited to within an inch of its life, you need a cover. With a print book, your cover has a front, a back and a spine. With an eBook, it has a front cover.

Is the cover important? Silly question. Despite the saying, "Don't judge a book by its cover," many people do. In fact, the cover can be the gatekeeper in a publishing house, the person who lets in your manuscript or pops it in the Return to Sender pile.

Self-published novelists are sometimes branded as amateurs with the word being used in the pejorative sense. This may stem from the presentation of their novel. Your cover can make or break it.

Some authors are good, even expert at graphic design and desk-top publishing. Why would they not design their own cover? Why not indeed? Then there are software programmes like Canva which provide templates for covers. So yes, a self-published novelist can create their own cover.

I'm not a graphic designer and I pay someone to do that job. The key to success is to (a) find the right designer and (b) give them a brilliant brief.

Find and help your designer

Here are some ways to locate the right person. Remember most will not read your novel, the blurb perhaps but not the book itself.

Look at book covers. There are hordes of examples online. If you are impressed, find out who designed it. Ask an online writing group of self-published authors. Who do you recommend? Search for relevant freelancers e.g. on fiverr search for book cover designers

Remember budget may be important to you and choose accordingly.

Finding the right designer is ideal but giving them poor advice will hurt. You're shooting yourself in the foot. I make a mock-up of the cover which I send to the designer. Give them as much information as possible, e.g. you want the main character to dominate.

As you saw earlier, the mock-up I sent to the designer of *All Their Christmases* was, I think, significantly upgraded to the finished product. You don't want to request correction after correction because the designer can't read your mind. They need your input.

I often have minor corrections such as a word or words not being in italics when they should be. But because I provide so much detail and a mock-up, it gives the designer free rein. It's better to give your designer too much information than not enough.

Photos

Many book covers have a photo or photos. I search for the one or ones I like. Be aware of copyright. Simply downloading a photo you fancy could land you in hot water. Copyright laws may protect the material being used for commercial use. Get permission first or better still, choose a photo where there is no copyright or where your purchase or your designer's purchase allows you to use the material.

I choose a designer who has the right to use certain photos. The design fee includes payment for a certain photo or photos. Examine this site.

[Stock Images, Photos, Vectors, Illustrations and Videos | Enterprise | Depositphotos](#)

This is a site where I often search for relevant photos. You could purchase one or more and pay for the material or select a designer who can legally use material from this site.

Here is one of my covers designed by a professional. It is for an eBook. It is in full colour in the eBook version of this book although not so in this printed book.

Below is the cover for the print book. Because there is more work required to produce a front, back and spine, usually you will pay more than for the eBook cover. The front cover of an eBook is the same as the front cover of a print book.

Note how the designer has allowed the artwork to flow from the front cover, over the spine and onto the back cover. I like that.

On the back cover I include a photo of the author and the essential barcode which contains the ISBN, the International Standard Book Number. The blurb is on the top of the back cover and book reviews are beneath the blurb.

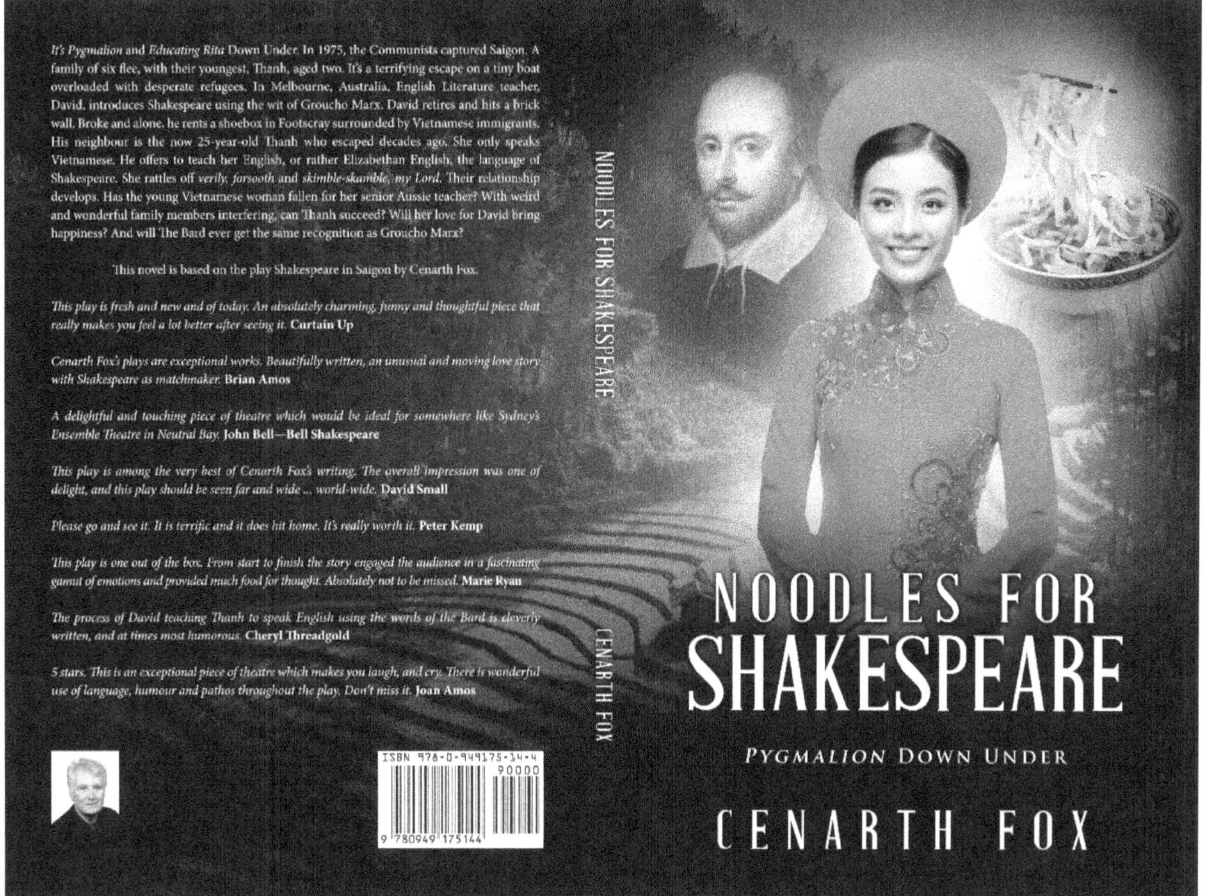

What about the title?

I choose a title from the off. I may not stick with it although usually I do. A working title is good. It gives your novel character.

Check to see you're unique. Pop your proposed title into a search engine and see what appears. If someone is using that title, seriously consider creating something else. Even a similar title could be confusing.

Are you famous?

Some novels written by a famous author see the novelist receiving major billing. On the cover, the author's name can be big even huge. It's easy to see why. Their books sell in massive numbers so the publisher wants to be sure readers know their star writer has written another (they hope) best seller.

If you're a first-time novelist I wouldn't be setting your name in 188-point type. Instead, do the following.

- ✓ Make sure you have a professional-looking cover
- ✓ Make sure it announces your genre
- ✓ Give your name a modest but never hidden appearance

The blurb

This is the description of your novel which usually appears on the top of the back cover of your printed novel or near the front of your eBook version. It's important. I'll say that again. Your blurb is important. People study the front cover then often turn to the back cover. That could be when they replace your novel and look elsewhere or open your book.

Wall sign 1 – 5 words
Elevator Pitch under 100 words
Blurb under 250 words (between 150 and 250)
A blurb is an extended Elevator Pitch and has four parts.

- ✓ Hook
- ✓ First Part
- ✓ Second Part
- ✓ Cliff-hanger

Hook speaks for itself. It's designed to hook the reader. Unlike an Elevator pitch, a blurb can feature names of characters. Try and slip your genre in early.
"In 1683, the young teenager …" Immediately we see it's an Historical Fiction novel.
Part 1 can include a dramatic or thrilling event, even life changing.
Part 2 develops the conflict.
Cliff-hanger – with no spoiler alerts.

What do the professionals write for their blurbs? Look through the novels in your collection, in your local library, in a bookshop. Learn from the pros.
Edit your blurb within an inch of its life.
There are many free videos online explaining blurbs.

More on Blurbs

Start with a hook. Why should the reader keep reading? One sentence is best. Always leave the reader wanting more.

It is NOT

- ✓ a plot summary
- ✓ a Table of Contents
- ✓ an explanation of a character/s
- ✓ a warning about part of the story (No spoiler alerts)

It COULD/SHOULD

- ✓ Evoke emotion
- ✓ Make the reader feel something
- ✓ Relate to other books/characters – you can reference a book readers may know
- ✓ Lead them to the CTA (the Call to Action) to purchase or borrow your novel

The layout of your novel

This is as important as your cover. Once the reader opens your novel, they see the layout. This includes several things.

- ✓ Choice of font
- ✓ Size of font
- ✓ Is it serif or sans serif?
- ✓ Does it have artwork such as a dropped cap?
- ✓ What space is there between lines?
- ✓ What is the space between sections?
- ✓ Is there artwork for new chapters?
- ✓ What are the margins?
- ✓ Chapter headings

Remember the font size in an eBook can be changed by the reader. They tap the screen on the reading device and choose **Aa** the icon for font. The pop-up allows the reader to change the size of the text. But obviously in a print book, the font size is fixed.

So, choose well because the choice of font is important. Look at the interior of some novels. Do you find them easy to read? Which font has been chosen? You should like the font in your novel which must be easy on the eye. You need to be proud of your novel, its content obviously but equally so its appearance. I like the font, Georgia.

Now we need to choose the font measurements. My recommendation for a book in the common size of 6 x 9 inches (15.24 x 22.86 cm) is as follows.

- ✓ 10.5-point font size
- ✓ 1.15 point as the distance between lines

This book in printed form has an A4 page size which is 8.3 x 11.7 inches or 210 x 297 cm. This book uses the Georgia font, with the basic text in 12-point, sub-headings in 16 point and chapter headings in 20 point. The space between the lines is 1.15.

The space between the lines is important. There is not much difference between 1 and 1.15 but readers appreciate the difference. It makes the text easier to read.

Fancy or plain

Another choice for the self-published author. Do you want a drop cap at the beginning of each chapter?

Londoners loved a good hanging and the more swinging stiffs the better. Rain, hail, or shine, in 1812 massive crowds flocked to the free spectacle with traders making a killing. *A Sweeping Saga* **Cenarth Fox**

An alternative to a dropped cap is to put the first word or words of a new chapter in caps. I've used a mixture in this book to help you choose. Normally you would use one or the other but by me using a mixture, it gives you a chance to compare.

A section is a break within a chapter where one scene ends and a new one starts. The reader needs to be told that fact. They can't be reading and involved in the story when some characters vanish without warning and different characters appear. You must tell the reader things have switched location, time, situation, etc. To do so, select a method. Some self-publishers put a simple gap, they hit Enter and a space appears. Some hit Enter twice for a larger gap.

Some make the break obvious by placing some artwork between the sections. Some even decorate the page with a whole picture appropriate to the story with the text set over the illustration.

Chapter headings are a chance to be fancy. You can drop the text down the page, use a larger and different font or keep it plain and simple.

These are decisions for the self-published author. Study novels, particularly those in your genre, and see what others have done. Do you like their choice? If so, apply such artwork to your novel.

Margins

These are super important with the paper, the print version of your novel.

A self-publisher can do just about everything on their own. They can edit, design and prepare the files for their novel to be published. Mind you it is wise to at least consider having others help. This could mean hiring a professional to design your cover and maybe even your layout.

But one thing you must get right are the margins of your page.

In a print book, the common form of binding is known as Perfect Binding. The cover is thicker than the pages which in sections are glued to the cover. The more pages in your novel, the more difficult it can be to read in the middle section. This is why your margins must be spot on.

Open a novel and look at the margins. The outside margins are narrower. But they too are important because the pages are trimmed after printing.

For my 6 x 9-inch novels, in Word under Layout, Margins, Custom Margins and Page Set up, I insert the following:

Top 2 cm   Bottom 2.2 cm
Inside 2.3 cm   Outside 1.5 cm
Orientation is Portrait
Pages is Mirror Margins
Apply to Whole Document

There is a preview graphic which enables you to see what the text looks like on the page. Play around with the figures and watch how the text moves on the graphic.

That preview graphic helps but there are some protection measures available. The company printing your book will send you a proof copy. This allows you to see any mistakes including margin errors. Request changes before giving the okay to print. You may incur a fee for changes. Prevention is better than cure so get things right first time.

Finally, you could order one copy of your new novel. Obviously, it will be more expensive per unit than if you ordered say 20, but with the printed novel in your hands, you can see the final look and presentation of your masterpiece, and then order multiple copies with confidence.

Chapter 11
Publish your Novel

IT'S GOOD TO KNOW about the four types of publishing. Knowledge is power.

- ✓ Traditional
- ✓ Vanity
- ✓ Hybrid
- ✓ Self

Traditional publishing is so-called because this method of business has been around for centuries. It was and still is the traditional way to create books. The writer, or their agent, approaches the publisher with an idea or manuscript and the publisher accepts or rejects the proposal. If they accept the work, the publisher provides a contract in which they take responsibility for every aspect of the novel's publication. In return, the author receives a percentage of the income from the sale of the book. There may even be an advance to the author. If the book sells well, it's likely the publisher will be keen to receive further manuscripts from that author. There is no financial contribution from the novelist.

The word *vanity* in vanity publishing is used in a pejorative sense. It refers to the author being vain. Their book is not accepted by a traditional publisher because it is poorly written or has little or no commercial potential. The author pays a vanity publisher to publish their book. You can ask, 'Why would a vanity publisher promote a novel when they have already been paid? What's in it for them?' Good questions. There are warnings about not dealing with vanity publishers who can charge a significant fee.

Hybrid publishing, not as old as both traditional and vanity publishing, fits between the others. Hybrid means something created by combining different elements. In a hybrid car, the elements are petroleum and electricity. A hybrid publisher, distinguishing itself from a vanity publisher, offers to publish an author's book in a deal in which the hybrid publisher and the author share the costs of production. This can still require the author to stump up a significant amount. Some hybrid publishers have a contract which seems longer than *War and Peace*.

Speaking of money, traditional publishers pay the costs with the novelist contributing nothing financially. With self-publishing, the novelist pays all the costs but has total control over the publishing.

As discussed, this book concentrates on self-publishing. You write the novel. You publish the novel. You can pay or co-opt others to help with aspects such as design, editing and marketing, etc. It's your call. But you, the author and self-publisher are in charge.

We concentrate on two publishing options – print and eBook. An audio book is a third option. A print book can have a hardcover or a soft cover sometimes called a paperback.

eBooks

The *e* stands for electronic which can be written as e-book or ebook.

There are advantages when you publish your novel in eBook form. For you, the novelist, there are no printing or postage costs. Some platforms may charge a delivery fee which can be as low as a few cents. If you discover a mistake or wish to make a change to your content, fixing the problem is a simple task. You publish an eBook by uploading the files (one for the cover and one for the text) to the platform you choose, again in a short and simple procedure. Amazon walks you through the steps which can be taken in a few minutes. Other platforms include Ingram Spark, Kobo, Smashwords, Lulu and Barnes and Noble.

While the uploading task is short and straightforward, you want to make sure you get it right. Don't rush answering the questions. Choosing the right keywords or phrases to attract the right readers is vital.

For the reader, eBooks are usually cheaper, sometimes much cheaper than printed books. Once bought, they can be delivered instantly.

eBooks can be sent to editors, writing buddies, publishers and readers with a few clicks of your mouse or taps of your pad.

Must my novel become an eBook?

No, but if readers love eBooks and millions own a Kindle or other device which stores eBooks, why deny them the chance to buy and read your novel? Why deny yourself becoming popular or more popular?

How my novel file becomes an eBook

The two most common ways are to hire a professional or DIY i.e. Do It Yourself.

There are hundreds of people who can convert your Word or Mac file turning it into an eBook file. Search for a freelancer on fiverr.com, someone who is experienced in this skill and has a high rating in the 5-star system. Their fee can be a deciding factor too.

Look for written reviews of this freelancer's work. Contact them by email, explain what you have e.g. a 50,000-word novel in MS Word (or whatever), and ask them for their quote and the time they require. Amazon like receiving the EPUB version of an eBook.

Ask around a writing group, your writing group. Can anyone recommend a freelancer who will convert your novel? Good recommendations from word of mouth can reap rewards. There may be someone in your community, club or church who can help.

When looking for a freelancer, fiverr.com is a good place to start. Once you've joined the site, search for *Create an eBook* or *MS Word file to an EPUB eBook.*
Fiverr | Freelance services marketplace | Find top global talent

Here's an alternative. Software programmes can do the job for you, e.g.
DOC (WORD) to EPUB (Online & Free) — Convertio
This free software has converted millions of .doc files turning them into EPUB files, into eBooks. Most Word files now are .docx. You need to convert those files into a .doc file.

There are several books which take you through the process of converting your novel into an eBook. I used a book *From Word to eBook* by Ben Macklin, available from Amazon.

His method requires two pieces of software. The first is Notepad, a text editor which is free to all Windows users. The equivalent is TextEdit for a Mac.

The second required piece of software is Calibre. calibre - E-book management. This becomes your library of eBooks and is the software which turns your .doc file into an EPUB. It is free to download and comes with a video tutorial. Click on DEMO.

Once you have Notepad or TextEdit and then Calibre, you should be good to go. Remember you have choices when converting your file to an eBook.

- ✓ create the eBook yourself using the Ben Macklin book method below
- ✓ use Convertio free software to have it done * (See below)
- ✓ persuade someone with expertise to do it for you or
- ✓ pay a freelancer to do it for you. You could use fiverr to find a freelancer

* DOC (WORD) to EPUB (Online & Free) — Convertio They claim to have converted some 27,000 million files.

Once you have an EPUB version of your eBook, (or other versions such as MOBI) you can upload it to Amazon and tell the world your novel is available for download.

The Ben Macklin method is not the only one available. It's based on his eBook *From Word to eBook* available from Amazon. Here's the link.
from WORD to EBOOK: a step by step guide to formatting and creating an eBook from WORD eBook: Macklin, Ben: Amazon.com.au: Books

Once you have your EPUB file, test it on the free Amazon viewer. Make sure all the links work and it looks A-okay. Uploading instructions follow in this chapter.

What about a print version of my fabulous book?

As a novelist, you surely want to see your work in print. But if you're a beginner, should you find a commercial printer and order a dozen or maybe fifty copies? I would say, no. Start small. If you have a home office and printer, you could make your own single copy. This will place a printed book in your hands. You can read your novel other than on a screen. A common paper size for a home office is A4. I would have two columns per page, choose 10.5 point as the size of your text with a 1.15 space between lines. Print your novel on both sides.

A substitute printed book

You can set up your novel in either portrait or landscape orientation. A staple in the top left corner will do or you could have a coil binding down the left margin.

There are many instant print places. Depending on the size of your novel – remember in this course we are aiming for a word count of between 40K and 50K which is not huge.

You'll have an A4 page with two columns of text. Double-sided printing. Spiral binding on the left. Your cover is printed single-sided. Save your file as a PDF to a USB stick with your cover as the first page. Some instant print stores will accept your file by email and, for a fee, will deliver the finished product.

Hey presto, you have a print copy of your masterpiece.

Finally, a professional printer of books

There are many of these businesses and you should do two things.

- ✓ Triple-check your files before you choose a printer
- ✓ Question the printer from written questions you've compiled

There's no worse feeling than having told the printer to hit PRINT then to receive your new novel and find it has errors or doesn't look right. This problem is overcome with a Proof Copy.

The printing business sends you a copy of your files electronically – the cover and the text. You should take your time and go over the Proof Copy with an eagle eye and note any mistakes or changes you require.

WARNING: You may have to pay for corrections which is why your proofreading must be perfection plus. Still, it's better to remove the errors before the books are printed.

Be sure to engage the right printer. If they specialize in wedding invitations and political flyers, you may be in the wrong place. You need a printing business which prints books.

Chat with them, in person or on the phone. Study their web page. Write your questions and write your answers when they reply. If visiting their business, ask to see samples of books they have printed. Get a quote. Be sure you know what you want. What size is your novel? Is your cover to appear in colour? What is the process the printer uses?

The book will probably be printed in sections, usually 4, 8 or 12 pages each. If your interior – you don't count the cover – has 144 pages, you'll finish the printing on the last page. But if the company want the last page to be blank so they can add their own ID, your total page count will be 145 pages. If they are printing 12 up, that leaves 11 blank pages at the end. Ask the printer about the number of pages per section. Trust me, you don't want a collection of blank pages at the end.

Either reduce the number of pages or fill the blank pages with information about your other novels. What other novels? At least be aware of this situation.

You could save shoe leather speaking to a few printers by phone. Do they have a web site? Study it and notate your questions.

How do you find the ideal printer? One way is to ask fellow writers who are self-publishers. Who did they use? Were they happy with the result? Recommendations from happy customers is a good way to go.

A printer and a distributor

There are printing businesses which agree to promote your novel on their web site once they've printed your work. You need to choose a print business which you believe is right for you. Study these topics.

- ✓ The quality of their printing and binding
- ✓ The cost of their work
- ✓ Their ability to promote your novel

One printer I have used is Ingram Spark. They offer more than a printing service. At no cost they can place your novel on their list of available books. Ingram Spark claim to have contact with 45,000 libraries and bookshops worldwide. If you have Ingram Spark print your novel, you can sign up to their free distribution programme.

IngramSpark: Self-Publishing Book Company | Print & Distribute

This is a serious way to market your books. Buyers can enter bookshops around the world and request your novel. The retailer finds it in Ingram Spark's catalogue and places an order for the customer. Your novel can be printed and delivered within a short time. If you're communicating with someone who shows an interest in your novel, unless you have a copy in your swag, you can direct them to a local bookshop.

The biggest

Amazon is a giant in the publishing business and offer novelists different ways to promote their novel. More on Amazon in this chapter.

Audio books

This is a third option for self-publishers and a rapidly growing one. Amazon offers a programme called Audible. To see how popular audio books have become, look at Audible titles and the number of reviews given to many novels. There are audio books with thousands even tens of thousands of reviews.

The audio book market is worth billions and predicted to increase in the future.

There are many articles on how a self-published author can convert their novel to an audio book. I recommend you study the topic in detail. If taking responsibility, you'll need a narrator and recording venue, and once the narration is complete, as with print and eBook versions, you'll need a platform from which listeners can obtain a copy.

Self-publishing a print and/or eBook may require a much lower financial investment.

Amazon and eBooks

It's the biggest. It accepts your novel to be printed, and your converted file as an eBook. Uploading your novel to Amazon, (print or eBook) I've found to be straightforward, and the eBook can be available within days, even hours. Here are some uploading suggestions.

Signing up to Amazon

1. kdp.amazon.com (Create an account)
2. Click **Bookshelf**
3. Click **Create**
4. Select (a) **eBook** (b) **paperback** or (c) **hardcover**
5. Let's assume you choose **eBook**

Language	English
Title	As on your book cover – no variation
Sub-title	Only if you have one. Don't use it to bump up keywords
Series	For now, ignore
Edition No.	If you later make changes, you must advise potential readers*
Author	You or your pen name
Contributors	If you've done everything, add nothing. If designer, add their name.
Description	It appears on Amazon and is important. You could use your blurb.

You can format your text – use bold, italics or HTML. Refer to Amazon guide – *How do I format the description?*

*Notes: let's say you upload your eBook and then find an error in your novel – heaven forbid. You make the change and upload the new version. Even if it's only one word, you must tell potential readers this is Edition 2 or whatever. Solution: don't make errors.

Publishing rights ✓	I own the copyright
Primary audience	Choose **No.** Why? Because there are no explicit sexual images on cover or inside
Reading age	Only if it's a book for children
Primary marketplace	**Amazon.com** is the US and it has about 330 million people but **Amazon.com.au** might be better if your book is about indigenous Australians. I use **Amazon.com**
Categories	There are sub-categories e.g. History – American
Keywords	Super important. Read *How do I choose keywords?* A keyword can be a phrase. Never try and trick Amazon
Release date	**Yes** because you only fill out this page once your book is ready to go

The following data appears on Amazon page 2

DRM	DRM stands for Digital Rights Management and KDP says it is "intended to inhibit unauthorized access to or copying of digital content files." Thieves will always find a way to steal. It may hinder your sales. But I advise you do NOT tick the box but understand you cannot change your decision. It is one example of not being able to change something.
Manuscript	Upload manuscript as EPUB file
Cover	Upload cover preferably as JPEG
AI use	No, assuming you haven't used AI in producing your novel.
Preview book	Launch their previewer - the link is on page 2 on their site.
ISBN	Not needed for an eBook ASIN - Amazon Standard Identification Number provided by Amazon

----

The following data appears on Amazon page 3

KDP Select	Allows you to offer discounts and offer free books. I recommend you take this option. See below under **Price**
Territories	Select All Territories
Primary Market	You chose that on Page 1. I choose **Amazon.com**
Royalty	I choose royalty of 70%
Price	Must be between US\$2.99 and US\$9.99 For most of my novels I choose US\$2.99. Why that figure? (a) it's not a big book and (b) to attract more buyers If you're in KDP Select, you get 5 days every 3 months to offer a discount and even a free copy
Check	Triple check everything then hit *Publish your Kindle eBook* It can take 72 hours for your book to appear Sometimes it takes 12 hours

KENP stands for Kindle Edition Normalised Pages. It caters for people who borrow rather than buy an eBook. Amazon calculates the number of pages read by a Kindle Unlimited subscriber. You earn royalties for every page of your eBook a reader reads. Amazon determines the amount month-to-month. You may not make a fortune but every little bit counts.

Congratulations! Don't spend all your royalties at once. And don't forget to enrol your eBook in KDP Select.

Chapter 12
Market Your Novel

Many novelists, me included, love writing but are less keen on marketing. In fact, less keen for some could be replaced by hate or loathe. Well, tough, because it's a fact that self-published authors must do their own marketing; must do everything.

That last bit is not true. You can employ people to help in different ways, even in marketing. There are freelancers who, for a fee, will promote your book in many and varied ways. Explore "Book marketing" on fiverr.com.

But it's pointless pouring all your energies into creating your book and then doing little or nothing to tell the world it exists. So, buckle up and promote your novel. Try these ideas.

- ✓ Paid ads
- ✓ Free ads
- ✓ Personal appearances
- ✓ Book blogs and competitions
- ✓ Free or reduced prices
- ✓ Lead magnet
- ✓ Local radio and newspapers
- ✓ Book launch
- ✓ Web site
- ✓ Create a list

A word of warning from the off. There are many platforms, outlets and businesses willing to take your hard-earned cash in return for promoting your novel. Let the buyer beware. ROI or Return on Investment should dominate your thinking. Promises cost nothing but can come with side effects with possible surgery required for your hip pocket. I suggest you start small, study the results and invest money wisely, if at all.

When marketing at first, I recommend you use as many free avenues as possible. Certainly, paying for promotion can be beneficial but saving money is a winner at least when you start marketing. Here are the details of your marketing possibilities.

Paid ads

Giants like Facebook, Amazon, BookBub, Google and Goodreads are places to consider. Then there are specialist book promotion sites such as Book Adrenaline, Book Dealio, Book Doggy, Voracious Readers Only and Bargain Booksy. Take your time and check out their services.

Free ads

You can't argue with the price. Facebook will run your paid ads, but you can promote your novel on your own FB page as well as on X, Instagram, Tik Tok and others. Sensible articles or posts only please. See WARNING below.

There are pages for groups on these social media giants which specialize in novels. Look for groups which relate to your novel. Join them. This way you'll see what others are posting and allow you to respond. There are groups dealing with crime, historical fiction, romance, children's literature, sci-fi, fantasy and others. Making a sensible and relevant posting is free and a way of introducing yourself and your novel.

WARNING

A major no-no in marketing is to say, "Buy My Book!" The world is full of novels and one way to lose credibility and to not make sales is to adopt an aggressive or me-me-me stance. Give to receive. By providing information or material which is interesting, helpful and free establishes you as a kind person who can be trusted, and hopefully a genuine novelist. Readers respond to novelists who care about others. Giving fellow novelists and readers a tip or information on what you found helpful is always welcome.

Personal appearances

This can be a low priority for some novelists because of their reluctance to speak in public. Think it through. Write your speech and practice reading it. This should remove any concern about "drying". Make a Power Point presentation meaning your audience will look at the screen and not at you. Talk about each new slide when it appears.

Who will book an unknown writer? Many groups particularly retirees. Probus clubs and retirement villages book speakers all the time. Libraries book authors. Give yourself a gimmick. Take the theme of your novel and create your talk around that theme. You will have done some research on the topic before writing your novel. Use the information you discovered and pitch your talk accordingly. I've given an illustrated talk about Sherlock Holmes for 20+ years.

Of course you don't have to say, "Buy My Book!" because your talk should/will create interest. Always have copies to sell, as well as free promotional material. You can have a business card, and many novelists have a bookmark printed with the cover of their novel, web address, email, etc. Have them available for interested listeners.

Remember too that having the ability to accept plastic can mean the difference between achieving a sale or not. There are devices which work via your phone enabling you to accept card payments.

Be prepared to think on your feet. I have several series of novels and at a book fair and other events, and if someone shows an interest in a whole series, I give them a discount there and then. And it doesn't have to be a series. If the novels are $20 each and the customer showed an interest in more than one book, I would offer three novels for $50.

Book blogs and competitions

Get to know book bloggers. They love books, often write fiction, and have a blog with book-related articles. Many welcome guest bloggers. If you have a relevant article, you can suggest the topic and, if accepted, your article along with your name and web site details or novel title will appear and could be read by hundreds even thousands of readers.

Many bloggers offer competitions. Offer your novel as a prize. Readers enter. The downside can be if the blogger wants print copies meaning overseas postage might be a factor. If they take eBook versions of your novel, there is no cost. Remember the internet means writers and readers live all over the globe and can be contacted online.

Apart from the publicity the competition provides for your novel, you will get the email address of the winner/s, and hopefully everyone who entered. Add names to your list.

Free or reduced prices

If you upload your novel to KDP, Kindle Direct Publishing, part of Amazon, you are given the option of offering certain deals. You can offer your novel for free or for a reduced price. You are allowed to do so for five days every three months, and this is another way to stimulate interest in your book. Join KDP Select, a free service for Kindle eBooks.

Lead magnet

This is where you offer something for nothing to obtain the name and email address of a reader. If you've written your first novel, giving it away might get you contact details for future readers but nothing in the way of sales. If you have a series of novels, you can offer Book 1 and hope that encourages readers to buy the others in your series.

For a one-novel author, you could offer the first three chapters of your novel. Put them with your cover in a PDF and offer it in exchange for the readers' name and email address.

WARNING

Always mention how names and email addresses are never revealed to anyone. Building a reputation as a trusted author is essential. Readers may never have heard of you and need to feel safe giving you their private information.

Local radio and newspapers

Newspapers today are often digital or a hybrid with a print and digital version. Local newspapers still exist and local or community radio stations are everywhere. Both radio and newspapers constantly want material. As a local novelist you qualify.

If there is an entertainment section or a book programme, contact these media outlets with a simple flyer. *Local author publishes first novel.* Or second or third or latest novel.

Include a picture of your stylish cover and your EP, your elevator pitch. Obviously include your contact details and if you haven't heard from the outlet after a few days, telephone them asking if they have received your missive. Polite but persistent is your approach.

And have a cheat sheet to hand if they call you for an article or a live interview. Make a list of all the things you need to say about your novel. It's frustrating if the interview ends and you realize you haven't mentioned one or more important facts.

Book launch

Your novel is ready and to make immediate sales, have a book launch. What do you need?

- ✓ Venue
- ✓ Invitations
- ✓ Publicity
- ✓ Refreshments
- ✓ Cash and card facilities
- ✓ Guest speaker
- ✓ BOOKS

You invite friends, Romans and countrymen. People come to support you but also for the refreshments and because it's a social event. The venue is important. If you invite many and most arrive, some with a plus one, your back garden may be too small. A local hall, sporting pavilion or library could do. But you don't want guests parking a mile away.

"Early to bed, early to rise, it's no jolly good if you don't advertise." It's an old saying but you don't want to throw a party and have no-one show up.

Refreshments appropriate for the time of day are essential. You may be able to serve wine without a licence if you are not selling the liquor.

Always make the sale of your novel as easy as possible. Have a table with your books on display. A bigger poster, say A3, with your cover in all its glory will impress. You'll need a float, cash for change for cash buyers, and a device for taking plastic.

You do not sell the books. Have a friend or family member in charge of transactions. You are nearby ready to sign the purchased books.

I have a small notepad and two pens to hand. "Who is it for?" I ask the buyer. In most cases I write the name on the notepad first. This ensures I spell the name correctly. If someone has bought the novel for their partner, child, parent, etc., they don't want *To Alice* when it should be *To Elise*. I add something short such as *Happy reading*.

It's better to have someone launch your novel rather than do it yourself. Choose wisely. Does the person want to launch your novel? Have they read the book? Are they witty, a good speaker and keen to give your masterpiece the launch it deserves?

Finally, books. Placing an order for a thousand of your novels is probably crazy. No, it *is* crazy. But you don't want to make all those sandwiches and profiteroles, pull a crowd and have people with money in hand miss out because you've run out of books. Keep most of your novels out of sight under a table with a decent supply, neatly arranged in view. Top up the supply when required.

Web site

You need one. *But I've only got one novel. And I don't know how to build a web site or make changes to it.* Okay, these are natural reactions. But it's not expensive to have a one-page web site and it's not expensive to have someone create it.

Again, finding a freelancer who does this type of thing is not hard. If you join fiverr.com (it's free to join) and then search for *web site designers,* you will have more than enough possible creators. As usual, check out their previous work and the number of 4- and 5-star ratings. Once you find someone who looks the goods, have an online conversation.

Search for web sites run by self-published authors. Discover who designed their site. Do you like it? Contact the designer. My site is www.cenfoxbooks.com. Consider having a store on your site where you can sell your novel directly.

Learn how to make simple changes to the site. Let's say you get a positive review of your novel. Web sites are active. You could put this latest review on your site. Being able to do that yourself saves time and money.

"I have read all of Sir Author Conan Doyle's stories and when I find a story of Sherlock, I like I'm really, really happy. This story is fantastic. How great it would be if Sherlock and Watson were real. Two worlds collide and it is funny. Thanks Mr Fox." **Amazon** *Sherlock Holmes: Playing the Game*

Create a list

It's the best and cheapest way to market your novel. It's the last item in this chapter and the one with the greatest potential. It's what it says on the tin. You create a list of names and email addresses. These are people who read, especially if they read in the genre of your novel, and who want to hear from you about future novels.

Now I've already spoken about the need to protect a person's privacy. They are handing over their personal information and it is sacred. You do not reveal this information to anyone ever. Period. Full stop. And that fact is clearly stated for the would-be client.

Now think of the benefits. Through email, you have a direct link to a person who has given you their details because they are interested in your writing. This is a quality over quantity situation.

You can buy millions of email addresses and most, at best a miniscule fraction, are useful. Most are useless. You want people who read and preferably books in your genre.

How do you find them? Place an invitation on your web site. I have two lead magnets on the first page of www.cenfoxbooks.com. I offer two free novels in return for the visitor's name and email address.

Any flyer you send, any bookmark you print and give away, any talk you give, you promote your web site and lead magnet. This is one important way to build your list.

There are paid businesses like Mailer Lite and Mail Chimp. They offer ideas and ways to promote your novel and in return handle requests from anyone who clicks on your link.

Build your list and over weeks and months you keep adding new readers. Once you have their details, you need to keep in touch. Never bombard them with emails and when you do send something, make it interesting. Provide value for their investment in your work.

I send a newsletter whenever a new title appears. If you haven't got your next novel to hand, send a newsletter with news about what you're writing, reviews – good and not so good – you've received, and any other offers you have provided.

I made a five-page PDF with insights into the main characters in my 8-book series *The Detective Joanna Best Mysteries*. It has a photo of each character and their life story. It gives background information and other details not found in the novels. It doubles as a lead magnet to attract new readers but is a gift to keep those on the list aware of my work.

Build your list.

Dictionary for Novelists

allegory	a novel (poem or picture) with a hidden meaning
alliteration	adjacent words with same consonant at the beginning
allusion	implied or indirect reference to someone, thing
analogy	comparison between things to explain or clarify
antagonist	powerful character who opposes the protagonist
cliffhanger	a plot device where something dramatic and unresolved occurs at the end of a chapter, section or the book. Dickens and Conan Doyle stories were first published in magazine format and often ended with a cliffhanger moment. Readers became keen to buy the next edition to see what happened
climax	the strongest part of drama or tension in a story
dialogue	words spoken by characters
euphemism	a mild word or words in place of a word or rude, harsh words
flashback	part of the novel which happened before the present time
foreshadow	suggest, hint at something which will happen later
gatekeeper	a person who first encounters a manuscript sent to a publisher. The gatekeeper has the power to reject said manuscript before it even gets to first base
hyperbole	exaggeration to emphasize a point
irony	words which convey the opposite meaning to what is meant
KDP	Kindle Direct Publishing, major part of Amazon
Kill Your Darlings	Remove work you love because it doesn't suit your narrative
metaphor	figure of speech not to be taken literally compares different things, e.g. life is a rollercoaster. Unlike a simile and doesn't use *like* or *as*
onomatopoeia	the word sounds like the meaning of the word, e.g. buzz
paradox	it seems a contradiction but is true, e.g. less is more
POV	Point of View from which a story is told
protagonist	main or major character in your novel
Save the Cat	An incident which makes a character appeal to readers
simile	figure of speech comparing two things using like or as, e.g. Frank looked as big as a bear
personification	assigning non-human things with human characteristics
satire	to verbally attack people or society with humour or irony
theme	the basic message, meaning or moral of the novel
raison d'être	a French phrase meaning a reason for existence
3D	a character who is well-rounded with a heart is said to be 3D

Epilogue

If you plotted, wrote, edited and published a novel over an 11-week period, many congratulations. If you didn't finish on time, you too should be congratulated for achieving what you did. But don't stop. Keep going and finish your novel.

One theory about writing novels goes like this. The best way to learn how to write novels is to write novels. Once you started writing using the steps in this book, you learnt things. Every time you plotted, wrote or edited; you gained experience. Studying tips like *make it stronger not longer*, removing unnecessary words, and creating an elevator pitch and a wall sign, meant you gained knowledge and became a better writer.

If you haven't published your novel by the end of the book, I urge you to press on and do so. There is a great feeling of satisfaction when you get to hold your printed novel or see its listing as an eBook online.

You may try to find a literary agent to approach traditional publishers on your behalf. You may approach a traditional publisher to see if they will accept your work.

But get the order of business right. First try and find an agent. If unsuccessful, you could make a direct approach to traditional publishers. Don't do it the other way round. Agents might like your manuscript but won't be happy to learn it's already been rejected. Agents first, traditional publishers second.

You are free to approach hybrid and vanity publishers at any time but understand any contract with them will require you to make a significant financial contribution.

There are millions of people who self-publish and there are many free resources to help you do that. A list of resources follows in the next chapter.

A final word of encouragement. Your finished novel may not attract an agent or traditional publisher. Your finished novel is one of millions. But with self-publishing, it can be discovered and read. You will be a more interesting person once you publish your novel.

Keep reading. Keep learning. Keep writing.

Footnote

If you have any comments or questions, I can be contacted by email. I will be delighted to hear if you published a novel using this book. cen@cenfoxbooks.com

Resources

The following businesses and individuals were operating at time of publication. I have no connection with any other than being a subscriber or visitor.

Amazon KDP

http://kdp.amazon.com
The largest platform for self-published novelists. The most popular site on which to place your novel.

BookBub Blog

BookBub Blog - The book lover's inside source for news, tips, & deals
Major player in the self-publishing world with an emphasis on readers but then all writers are readers.

Bryan Cohen

BRYAN COHEN – Author. Podcaster. Coach.
Author teaching other authors about marketing and self-publishing.

Canva

Canva: Visual Suite for Everyone
Platform to help you design book covers, flyers, web sites and more.

Dale L Roberts

SelfPublishingwithDale.com
Self-published author and YouTuber with many videos.

David Gaughran

Writer Blog • Book Marketing Advice • Free Resources • David Gaughran
Huge range of books and videos for the self-published writer. Free newsletter

Deposit Photos

Stock Images, Photos, Vectors, Illustrations and Videos | Enterprise | Depositphotos
Site with vast number of graphics for use in cover design.

Derek Doepker

Derek Doepker
Blogger with expertise in email marketing, persuasive ad copy, blog content, and other forms of content marketing.

Derek Murphy

My Story - Creativindie

Author and artist with vast knowledge of writing and publishing. Much free advice.

Historical Fiction Company

The Historical Fiction Company | Historical Fiction

Has a blog, podcast, library and magazine for all things historical.

Jericho Writers

Jericho Writers – Getting you published

Paid subscription service offering a range of services including masterclasses, tutored courses and editorial services.

Joanna Penn

The Creative Penn. Writing, Publishing, Book Marketing and Making a Living with your Writing

As the author says on her site, "I'll share my lessons learned on how to write, publish and market your book — and make a living with your writing."

Kathryn Johnson

Home - Kathryn Johnson, LLC

Author, coach and teacher of writing novels.

Kindlepreneur

Kindlepreneur - Book Marketing for Self-Publishing Authors

Free courses and hundreds of articles teaching authors how to self-publish and sell their novel.

Laura's Books and Blogs

Laura's Books and Blogs - Writing tips, giveaways, reviews, essays, and more!

The website description says it all.

Malcolm Richards

Home - Malcolm Richards

UK author who writes series of novels and invites others to share his work. Free newsletter which is excellent for novelists who wish to improve their marketing skills.

NaNoWriMo

Welcome | NaNoWriMo

Mentioned elsewhere, this site brings writers together helping them set goals, meet other writers while offering events and incentives to finish their novel. It's free!

Reedsy

Reedsy: Find the perfect editor, designer or marketer | Reedsy

Huge site offering quality vetted professionals to work as editors, designers and marketers. Free material for authors with articles, videos and publishing tools.

Self-Publishing Made Easy Now

Welcome To Self-Publishing Made Easy Now!

A one-man band. Chris Baird has done it all and shares his experience and knowledge to help you find the right readers, create and market your book.

The Novel Smithy

Build Your Writing Toolkit. - The Novel Smithy

Many free resources including a free weekly newsletter to help novelists. An example of the material on offer re the POV in your novel is listed below.

4 Ways to Choose the Right POV for Your Novel - The Novel Smithy

The Write Practice

The Write Practice: Helping Writers Get Better Since 2011

A site to help authors improve their writing. Has resources listing writing software, tools and apps.

Udemy

https://www.udemy.com

An online school offering several courses for self-published authors.

Voracious Readers Only

Voracious Readers Only | Connecting Readers with Authors

A site for both readers and authors but for authors it provides marketing offers. As an author you click the link AUTHORS. The company offers ways to connect your novel with readers interested in your genre.

Writers Victoria

Welcome to Writers Victoria - Writers Victoria

Based in Victoria, Australia offers variety of resources including online and in person courses, writing and publishing advice, competitions and writing groups. Manuscript assessment is available. Fortnightly newsletter in which members receive 3 free ads a year.

YouTube

https://www.youtube.com

Video platform. Search for such topics as *How to Format a Novel, How to Create an eBook, How to Make an Author Website, How to Market Your Novel,* etc.

Quizzes

Here is a chance to discover how much you have learnt from this book. The questions you can't answer can prompt you to re-examine that topic and make yourself a better writer.

Test 1

1. What is POV and which POV are you using in your novel?
2. What is meant by Show Don't Tell?
3. What is DAD?
4. What's the difference between a 2D and a 3D character?
5. What must you do when you get an idea?
6. What does "Save the Cat" mean?
7. Who should you write for?
8. What are the three parts, all starting with P, of writing a novel?

Test 2

1. How do you remove formatting from your Word document?
2. What do we mean by formatting?
3. What are some benefits of having your book as an eBook?
4. Which eBook format is favoured by Amazon?
5. Ingram Spark is a printer and what else?
6. What is a hybrid publisher?
7. What is a vanity publisher?
8. Which comes first – approaching a traditional publisher or finding an agent?

End of Course Exam

Answer questions without reference to your notes. Answers on the following page.

1. Approximately how many words in [a] short story [b] novella [c] novel
2. What are the three parts of a novel?
3. What is pantsing?
4. Name the four formats of a book.
5. What does POV stand for? How many POV possibilities are there?
6. Why use Show Don't Tell?
7. What does Kill Your Darlings mean?
8. What is NaNoWriMo?

9. What word starting with *s* is relevant in writing novels?
10. What does ISBN stand for?
11. Why have a bar code?
12. List 6 genres of novels.
13. What is an elevator pitch?
14. In writing a novel, what is a wall sign?
15. What is a blurb? Where does it appear?
16. Explain Save the Cat.
17. Explain the difference between a 2D and a 3D character.
18. What should you do once you get an idea?
19. Explain serif and sans serif.
20. Name the four types of publishers.

Answers

Up to 7,500, up to 25,000, at least 40,000
Beginning, middle and end
Writing a first draft without a plot
Paperback, hardback, electronic and audio
First, second and third – there can be two versions of second person
Creates a more vivid picture of the scene
Removing writing you love but which is not helpful to the narrative
National November Writing Month
Subjective
International Standard Book Number
For retailers to keep records of their transactions
Romance, thriller, crime, historical, literary, children's, sci-fi, fantasy
A brief synopsis of your novel
A word or words to keep you on track, a mini elevator pitch
A synopsis on the back cover of your novel
An incident revealing a character to be one of the good people
2D has two dimensions, 3D has three and is more rounded
Notate and store it
Serif typeface has small additions on the end of letters, sans (without) serif does not
Publishers - traditional vanity, hybrid, self

Happy writing!

Some novel series by Cenarth Fox

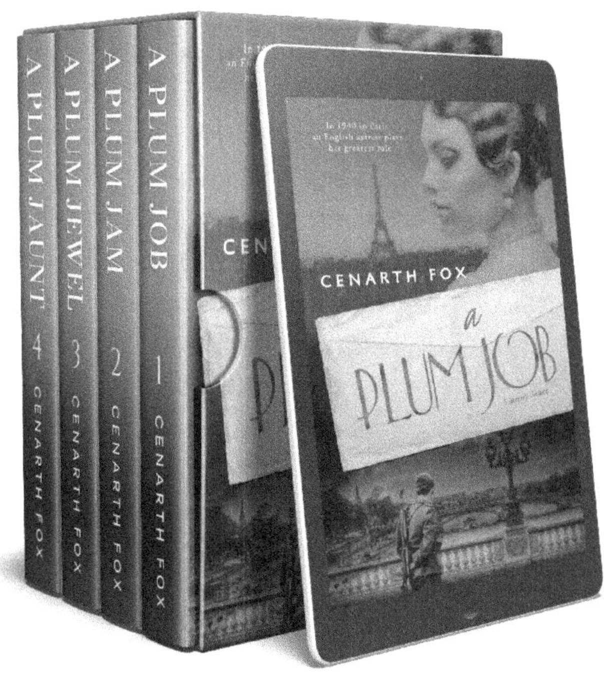

A brilliant, young English actress spies for her country in Nazi-occupied France. Churchill sends spies to set Europe ablaze. In war time Paris, Plum, real name Louise Beatrice Wellesley, clashes with the Wehrmacht, Gestapo, Resistance, gendarmes and an English double-agent. Her cover is an actress sharing a dressing-room with Edith Piaf and later as a nun in Lyon where some clerics hate the Nazis and others support them. Can the actress climb the Pyrenees to uncover a spy in Baker Street, London?

The young, new-kid-on-the-block, risk-taking homicide detective is Joanna Best. She is brilliant. Crims hate her as do some fellow cops. She works with IT genius, Michael, and Dr Gabrielle Strange, a well-named pathologist and chocoholic. The trio solve murders, fight evil people, devour chocolate, and hopefully appeal to crime fiction readers like you. Jo struggles with romance, loopy family members and mysteries at home and abroad. There are eight books in the series, the first is free.

More novel series by Cenarth Fox

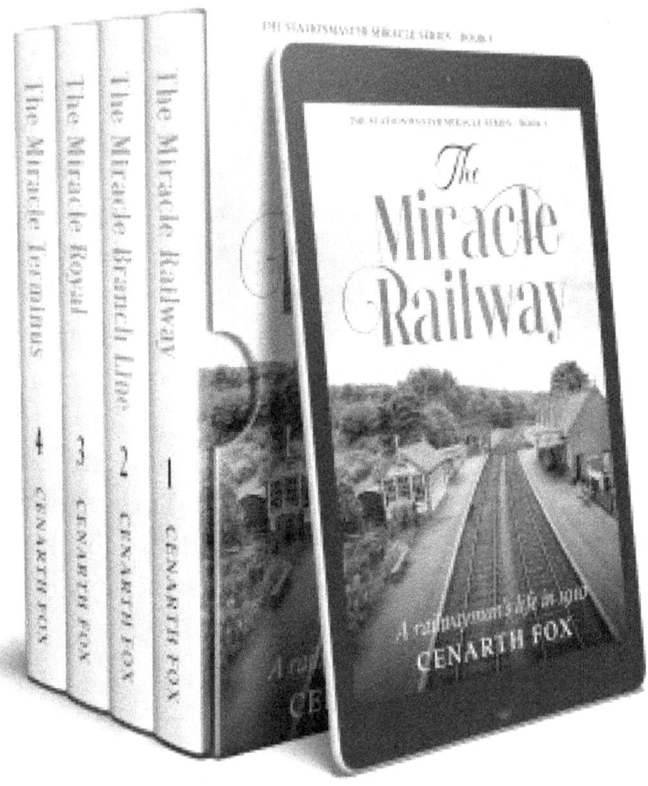

In 1910, 12-year-old George Miracle started as a station lad in London. His railway career lasted 50+ years. He swept platforms, lugged parcels, helped lost passengers, was arrested for murder, fought in a French trench in WW1, and became the youngest stationmaster in England. His branch line was dying. He fell madly in love and married in amazing venues. He tackled a crazy would-be murderer and armed robbers. Book 3 sees George the SM at the famous Royal Station, Wolferton. "Good morning, Your Majesty." He rises in the ranks and runs all UK trains during WW2.

Nicholas Twit is almost 11 with his bedroom a copy of the sitting-room at 221B Baker Street. With Felicity, 14, as Dr Watson, the pair tackle all manner of crime including lost cats and rubbish bin crooks. They use the methods Mr Holmes and Dr Watson used to solve mysteries. Apart from the tales, there are word games, new words and snippets about the world's greatest detective. Fully illustrated these novels are a brilliant way to introduce young readers to mystery fiction in general and to Sherlockian stories.

Standalone novels by Cenarth Fox

(Literary fiction with the Brontes, Agatha Christie, Conan Doyle and the Bard)

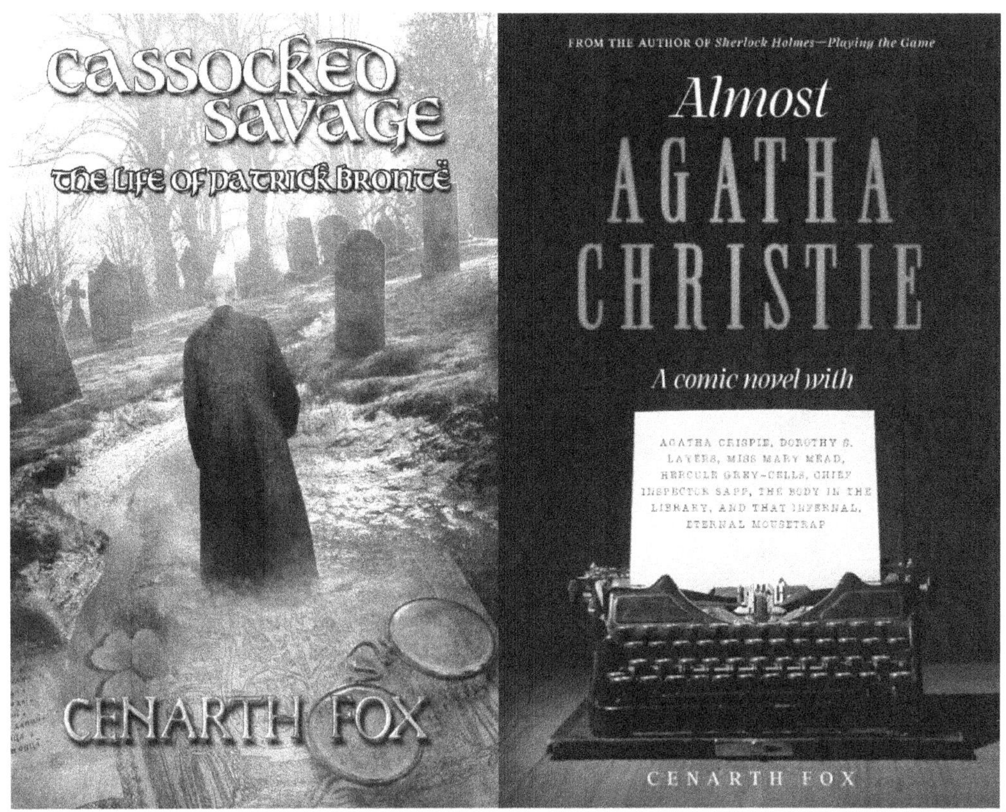

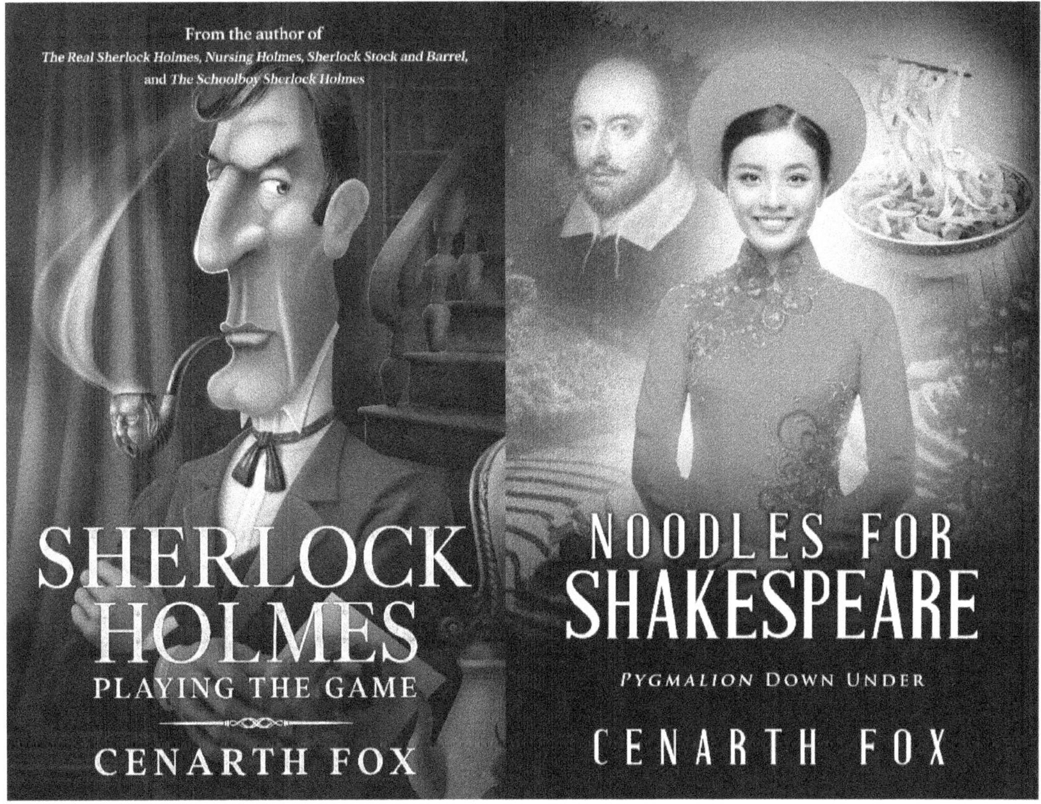

https://www.cenfoxbooks.com